VICTORIA

BY HANNAH HOFFMEISTER

BOOK 3 IN THE DREAM RING SERIES

You can do anything!
Hannah L. Hoffmeister
11-30-15

This novel is a product of the author's imagination. The events described in this story never occurred. Though localities, buildings, and businesses may exist, liberties were taken with their actual location and description. This story has no purpose other than to entertain the reader.

Published by Buttonwood Press
P.O. Box 716
Haslett, Michigan 48840
www.buttonwoodpress.com

ISBN: 978-0-9891462-1-0
Printed in the United States of America

I dedicate this book to my dad, who inspires me as he begins a new journey and follows his dreams. Thank you for all of your love and advice!

I also dedicate this book to the students I visited during the 2011-2012 school year. I enjoyed speaking to you about writing and achieving goals; I will cherish those memories forever!

ABOUT THE AUTHOR

www.dreamringseries.com

Hannah Hoffmeister is a sophomore in high school. Just like Ava and Victoria, she loves ice cream shakes and spending time with her best friends. Hannah enjoys traveling, cooking, writing, reading, and cheering for the St. Louis Cardinals.

ACKNOWLEDGEMENTS

I would like to thank my parents for always supporting me as I follow my dreams. I would also like to thank my siblings, Tom, Louis, and Norah, for their ideas, patience, and love throughout this process. Thanks especially to Grandpa and Nana Baldwin; I value your love and all that you have taught me, and it means a lot to me that you support my writing. I also need to thank my friends for believing in me, and Grandpa and Lesa Hoffmeister for always being there for me!

Thank you to the Buttonwood Press staff for their creativity and knowledge: Anne Ordiway, Editor; Joyce Wagner, Proofreader; and Sarah Thomas, Graphic Designer and Typesetter. I appreciate all of your suggestions and advice! Thank you to Matthew Fogle, Founder and Owner of SouthStar Studios, for all of your work on www.DreamRingSeries.com!

Thank you to Darlene Ederer, who welcomed me to her school and gave a great endorsement, and Emily Gregg, who motivates me with her enthusiasm. The book wouldn't be the same without both of you!

Chapter One

"Mom! Why not?" I asked. "Come *on*!"

"Absolutely not. You heard Nurse Norah."

"I'll be fine!"

"Ava, trust me—you need more time to recover."

Mom sat down at my desk and moved my wheelchair out of the way. She pulled her chair closer to me, settling in for this argument. I blew out a breath of frustration and said, "You want me to have my broom on Automatic the entire trip to Dream Ring while I sit on my bed in the cellar. That's certainly heroic."

"This isn't your decision. You aren't strong enough yet."

"Mom! I've been in bed for THREE MONTHS already. My concussion is almost fully healed, and I feel strong. I can stay awake as long as a normal person, and my back never hurts. Neither does my foot."

Okay—so that wasn't entirely true. My concussion wasn't healed, and sometimes I had horrible headaches, and my back… wasn't much better. I didn't want to tell Mom that it hurt whenever I tried to walk. But if this was what it was going to take to go to Neptune like a normal witch, I could lie. I would recover eventually.

"This matter is closed," Mom said coldly. She walked away from my bed, where I sat staring at my phone. Every once in a while I chatted with Kathryn, but mostly I was thinking about all of the fun times I had texting with my best friend Victoria. All of the inside jokes we had created, all the stress that she had taken away.

Now Victoria is being held prisoner on Jupiter. Widdidorm has been keeping her in that awful jail cell since we battled him last spring.

If Victoria were here, we would go over everything before heading to Dream Ring for the school year. Being a witch can be hard sometimes, but having your best friend by your side makes everything a lot easier. Being a witch targeted by her mother's ex-boyfriend who became evil is even harder. I would try to explain to Victoria what it was like for someone to hate you only because he wants revenge on your mother for something that was never her fault. Victoria would understand—she's the best friend I've ever had. And she's gone.

I rolled over in bed and wished I could have her with me right now. Even if I only saw her in a dream, that would help. The dreams are complicated. Sometimes I have these visions of

Victoria, except they're more like live video conferencing. Victoria can see me perfectly well; sometimes I can talk to her and sometimes I can't. As soon as I can, I'll go to Jupiter and rescue her. It's been hard enough not having her with me this summer. I won't let a whole year go by.

I was painfully easing myself into my wheelchair when Mom came into my room, worry lines creasing her forehead. "You have a phone call." She helped me into my wheelchair, noticing me wince a few times. I couldn't help it—it hurt my back, foot, and shoulder just to sit in that horrible contraption.

"Who is it?" I asked.

"It's Kathryn," she said. "Your friend from Dream Ring." *Well, duh. I don't know anyone else named Kathryn.* She handed me the phone and silently pushed me through the hallway and down the ramp Dad had built for me. She knew I had trouble wheeling myself with my bad shoulder.

"Hello?" I said into the phone.

"Hey," was her whispered response. "It's me."

"What's up?" I asked.

"Where are you?" she asked. "Can your mom hear me?"

"Yeah."

"Tell me when you have some privacy, okay?"

"Kat, you okay?"

"Uh… no."

Sensing I wanted to be alone, Mom wheeled me into our office and left.

"Okay, Kat. I'm ready."

"Is she gone?" she asked nervously.

"*Yes*. What's wrong?"

"I had a dream."

"Mmm-hmm."

"I saw Victoria."

"You *what*?" So far, I was the only one who had seen her.

Kathryn said, "She's not… well."

Last time I had seen my best friend—I had contacted her through a dream about three days ago—she had looked horribly underfed and dirty.

"What do you mean?" Kathryn wasn't coming across very clearly.

"She was speaking, but I don't know if she could see me. I think she was a little delirious, Ava."

"What do you mean, Kathryn!?" I asked, getting a little panicky.

"She was just talking, and somehow I connected into her dream. She was saying, 'An attack. He's planning an attack. An attack. I need help. I need help.' It was like she was in a trance or something."

"Are you making this up?" I asked. "She's never done anything like this."

"It's for real!"

"Then you know what we need to do, right?" The plan was obvious to me.

"Huh?" she asked.

"We have to get her."

"Huh?"

"Snap out of it, Kat! Here's the plan—you pick me up, you help me into your cellar, and we fly to Jupiter. If you want, you wait in the cellar while I rescue Vic. Then you take me to a hospital, and I'll be a hero."

"What?"

"Do I need to say it again?" I was frustrated. You would think that if someone felt the urgency to call another person and desperately tell her this information, she would be more on top of things. My fingernails flashed a pale yellow, and I tried to calm my irritated mood.

"No, no, I'm just thinking."

"Good. My throat hurts," I said. To tell the truth, so did my back.

There was a long pause. Then, "Ava?"

"Yes? Hey, Kat, I'm sorry I snapped. I just woke up from a nap."

"It's cool. I've thought about your idea, and I think it could work if we tweak it a bit. First of all, we should definitely go to Jupiter. I got bad vibes from this dream, and we need to rescue her soon. She's not, like, dying or anything, but she seriously needs medical attention. Second, we should bring another person. Two would be too risky. If we both fight Widdidorm, who's gonna take us to the hospital afterward or prevent us from getting captured like Victoria?"

"I'm on board," I said immediately. "Who should we take?"

"I propose Ella, but I'm open to ideas," she replied.

"Sounds good!" I said with a smile. "Next, please."

"Third, do we tell our parents? My mom might object." Kathryn had a point. My mom might object, too.

"I don't know," I admitted.

"If we need to contact someone, it would be a good idea to let them know, but then again, what if they try to keep us from going?"

"I know what you mean. I vote we tell our parents."

"Yeah, me too, I guess," she agreed.

"Anything else?" I asked. I was starving, and I could smell lunch cooking in the kitchen. My stomach growled.

"Not really. It's a simple plan, but it'll work. Are your powers full strength yet?"

"Almost. My fingernails are starting to glow again, and Mom has been giving me power-helping food at almost every meal. I'll talk to her and call you back in an hour or so, okay?"

"Yep! Talk to you soon."

"Bye!" I pressed 'end' on the phone.

"Mom?" I asked, painfully wheeling my wheelchair into the kitchen. She saw me wince and came over to help me. I really must give her credit for helping me so much. She knows that I still need the wheelchair and special attention, even though I insist I don't.

"Yes, dear?"

"I need to talk to you about Victoria. Kathryn had a dream about her. It was the first time anyone except me has seen her, so she called me. She said that Vic's kind of delirious, and we're both really scared for her. So we've decided to go rescue her. Tonight."

"Ava," Mom warned me in a motherly tone. "This might not be such a good idea."

"Let me finish! We'll bring Ella, too, so we'll have a third person. That way someone could help us fight, or," I took a deep breath and then spit out quickly, "take-us-to-the-hospital."

"What was that last bit?" Mom asked, smiling.

"Ha-ha. So, whaddaya think?"

"I don't know. I'm not ready for you to leave again. You can't even walk!"

"I can walk in the pool—at therapy," I offered.

"And how many pools are on Jupiter?"

"Yeah, yeah. Can we kick therapy up a notch, like, tonight?"

"Hold on, Ava. I have to make a call." And with that, she walked away.

"Oh, so the call is more important than me!?" I retorted at her back. She grabbed the phone and walked into her room, shutting the door behind her.

She came out moments later, holding several pieces of paper filled with scribbled writing. "Guess what?" she cried triumphantly. "I just found out something about the magical world that I never knew!"

"What?"

"Did you *know*," she mused, "that when you receive serious injuries on one planet, those injuries will heal if you avoid that planet for a certain period of time and then return? You qualify!"

"Wait," I commanded. "So I'll be fine on Jupiter, have my powers back?"

Mom nodded excitedly.

"*Yes*!" I cried. I pumped my arm—only once, though, because it hurt.

Mom grinned. "I'll help you pack, and then we'll pick up Kathryn," she said.

"What?" My voice was flat and not excited at all.

"Well, you need an adult chaperone," she said.

"No, no, *no*."

"Ava, it's dangerous!"

"*Mom*!"

She looked hurt. "What?" she asked.

My fingernails were as yellow as they could get without my powers being fully restored.

"Mom, you can help me pack. I admit, I can't do that alone. But you can't come with me to Jupiter. We agreed last year that this would be the way it happened. My friends and I have to do this. *Alone*. Come on, Mom. Please?"

Mom winced and closed her eyes, taking a deep breath. "I'll think about it."

We went to my room and began packing. Mom didn't say much, so I knew she was considering. This was good, this was good. When she went to the bathroom, I texted Kathryn to let her know that I was talking to Mom about the plan.

`All systems go. Working on her. U?`

She responded quickly.

`Mom is comin' around. Txt u l8r.`

Mom came back seconds later, and I snapped my phone shut. Mom tried to cover up her fingers, which were shining a mustard yellow; she was irritated.

"Honey," she started. "I really don't feel comfortable with you going to Jupiter alone."

"But—"

"Now, I'm still open to consideration. If you pitch a strong enough argument, then maybe I'll reconsider."

"Can't you just let me go? Why do I have to argue before I can save my best friend? Don't you realize how hard this has been on me? No Victoria down the street, no Victoria to text when I feel like crying, no Victoria to just *talk* to. Isn't that reason enough?"

Mom's face softened, and the lines around her eyes smoothed. "Yes, I know how hard it is," she told me. "Because Victoria isn't just *your* friend. She's like my second daughter. Having your second daughter captured and imprisoned isn't easy."

I felt bad for being so harsh. We finished packing in silence, and then Mom went downstairs.

Chapter Two

When I entered the kitchen, Mom was deep in thought, chopping carrots for tonight's stew. I quietly wheeled up to the table and played with a piece of clay left over from my art project last night, waiting for Mom to say something. It was about five minutes before she looked up and noticed me playing silently with the clay. "Hello, dear," she said, looking down at the carrots.

"Hi."

"I've thought about it."

"And?" I nodded my head at her as if saying, *Come on. I want to hear what you have to say.*

"You may go without a chaperone."

I breathed a sigh of relief, but at the same time, Mom coughed loudly. I realized that this was really a blessing, as there probably would've been a consequence if she thought I was being rude.

"I'm leaving tonight, then?"

"Well, your suitcase is packed, right?" she asked, eyebrows raised. And at that moment, Mom was less like my mother and more like a friend, someone I could joke and laugh with and talk to. I hadn't felt like this since Victoria was with me. It felt nice just to have someone be completely there for me, even if she was, like, thirty years older. We began chatting, just easy talk, and it felt good. This was a nice way to leave Earth. Not like last time, when Victoria and I had just up and left, not having enough patience to talk to her. This way was much better.

Mom handed me the phone and I dialed Kathryn's number. "All systems go," I said into the phone. "You?"

"Check," was all she said. "What time do we leave?"

"Midnight," I replied. "I'll pick you up at your bedroom window. Then we'll go to Ella's house, 'kay?"

"Sounds good."

"See you then! Oh, and Kathryn? Bring lots of first-aid stuff, power-helping food, magic textbooks, and whatever other junk you think will help."

"Um, okay! See ya!"

"Bye!"

Next I called Ella. She answered the phone, lazily saying, "What's up?" I had called her on her cell.

"Not much," I answered. "You?"

"Ava!" she shrieked. "I haven't heard from you since *May*! Oh my gosh, girl, how *are* you!?"

Last time I checked, I wasn't *this* close with Ella. But I guess I was open to the possibility of change. Maybe I had just been wrong about her the whole time.

"Whatcha doing?" I asked, twirling a strand of hair around my finger and making faces at Mom. She laughed.

"Nothing. Mama's at work, and I'm on the couch watching reruns of old shows. My little bro's on the phone with a friend chatting about video games. You?"

"Oh, just planning a rescue mission to get my BFF back from Jupiter," I said, like it was no biggie.

"That's more exciting than my story by far. Whatcha callin' for?"

"Well... do you want to come with Kathryn and me to rescue Vic? It'll be an adventure if nothing else."

The line was silent for a while. "Ella? You still there?"

"Oh," she said, sounding as if she had been really distracted. "Yeah. I'm thinking. Hey, could I call you back?"

"Sure."

"Okay, bye—wait! When do we leave, if Mama says yes?"

"Midnight. Kathryn and I will pick you up."

"Gotcha. Bye!"

"See ya!"

Well, it hadn't gone exactly as planned, but who knows? Maybe she had just changed from the last time I had seen her.

I watched TV for a while, sitting in the stiff wheelchair and wishing I could curl up on the couch.

The phone rang a half hour later. "Yo, Ava?"

"Hey."

"I can go!" She sounded pumped.

"Great! Is everything okay?"

"Yeah, totally. I'll see you at midnight!"

"It'll probably be more like twelve-thirty since I have to pick up Kathryn first."

"That's fine. What should I bring?"

"Food—power-helping food—your wand, spell-books, first-aid stuff, and any other magical junk you want to bring."

"Sounds good. Bye!"

"Bye!"

I wheeled up the ramp to think about our strategies.

Hours later, we were ready to leave. Earlier in the day, I had said goodbye to Dad without him knowing it. I just gave him a hug and told him that I loved him. He responded, "I love you, too, Ava." I wanted to cry when I heard the love in his voice.

Mom helped me climb out of the window and onto my broom. It was painful, and I winced and cried out. I told myself that Victoria was probably in more pain than me and that I was going through this for her. Mom pressed her lips into a thin line and looked as if she wanted to tell me that I couldn't go. Thankfully, she restrained herself and got on her flying carpet. She would accompany me as far as Ella's, but after that we would be on our own.

"Hey, girl!" Kathryn said excitedly, hugging her mom and getting on her broom. She silently glided through the window.

"Hey!" I responded.

She floated next to me, noticing my imbalance on the broom. "Are you okay?" she asked worriedly.

"Totally. Don't mention it." Mom looked like she was going to say something but didn't.

Next, we picked up Ella. She looked back at her house longingly and then set her mouth in a determined line, looking a lot like my mom. I laughed, and she looked at me curiously.

"Nothing," I said, giggling.

Mom gave me a hug after we left Ella's house. "Come back if something happens. I support you and I love you. Please be careful."

"Love you too," I said, pressing my face into her shoulder. She squeezed me and glided out of sight on her magic carpet.

"Well, girls!" I said cheerfully to them. "Are you ready to *save* the *day*!?"

"Whoop, whoop!" Kathryn added.

"Oh, *yeah*!" was Ella's response.

We chatted constantly as we rode out of Earth's atmosphere.

"Let's head to bed, girls," I said when I began to fight drowsiness. Flying on a broom while you're sleepy is never a good idea. We were just exiting Earth's atmosphere, but I was already pretty tired. "Hey, wanna camp out in my cellar?"

"Whoop, whoop!" was their response, a common reply so far.

They climbed carefully off their brooms and into my cellar. The small room expanded to three twin beds, a sink, and a chair.

"Where's the bathroom?" Ella asked.

"In the spell-book." Seeing their puzzled looks, I explained, "We have to use a spell to make a portable toilet. If you've ever wanted to try out your skills as a masterful plumber and handy-woman, the time is now."

"Don't think I'm doing this because I want to be a masterful plumber," Ella said, laughing, "I'm doing this because I know you can't." She took her wand from her purple robe pocket. Underneath she was wearing a long, white T-shirt that had rainbow stripes all over it and said, "WFF—Witch Friends Forever", and lime green leggings that looked super stretchy. On her feet were green and pink Nikes, and her hair was twisted artistically into a bun and had a pencil stuck through it. This was probably the most creative I had ever seen Ella.

"What's the spell?" she asked.

Kathryn turned to the "Miscellaneous Spells" chapter and recited the spell.

After the portable toilet was formed and we had all taken a turn, we banished it into hiding temporarily. Playfully, I stole the spell-book from Kathryn.

"Let's see if I can do a spell."

I scanned the long list of spells until I came to one that sounded interesting. "Collapserita Muscularanarium." My wand was aimed at Ella, just for fun. She didn't seem scared.

All of a sudden she collapsed. All the color was drained from her body and she looked sunken and shattered. Her head lolled and her eyes rolled. On inspection, she wasn't breathing. Uh-oh. Adrenaline raced through my body as I began to panic.

Then I saw a slight rise in her chest. *Phew*!

Slowly she came back to normal. "What did you *do* to me!?" she asked, looking exhausted.

I read the spell description. "'This spell collapses all muscles, hence making the phrase 'do not move a muscle' true. In most mortals this is impossible. If used in the wrong circumstances, this could kill a witch or wizard. Some witches have an extra half-lung that never stops breathing, no matter what the heart—a muscle—is doing. WARNING: DO NOT USE THIS SPELL WITHOUT CONFIRMATION THAT THE PARTICIPANT INDEED HAS A THIRD LUNG.' Oops."

Kathryn looked troubled. "Oh my *GOODNESS*, Ava! You just collapsed Ella! Good thing your powers aren't all healed yet or she might've died."

I realized that she was right. That had been *way* too close. It was obvious that Ella did not have a third lung.

"You can do a free spell on me," I volunteered. "I am so, so sorry—are you sure you're okay? Kat, please get Ella some power-helping food."

She scurried to her suitcase and pulled out a cinnamon bagel. She tossed it to Ella, who stuffed it into her mouth all at once, her eyes bulging when she realized her mouth couldn't hold the giant pastry. I pounded her on the back, and a slobbery bagel popped out onto the floor. "*Sick*!" I yelled.

"Sorry," she said, acting more like the Ella that I knew at Dream Ring.

"Can I do a free spell?" she asked, looking interested.

"Yep. My requirements are that they can't be potentially harmful or dangerous. No slumber-iumptia, either."

At the mention of those dangerous words, my wand vibrated a bit. I closed my hand around it as if I could calm the magical wood.

"Okay."

Ella looked at the spell-book, which I noticed was open to the "Miscellaneous Spells" chapter. This would not be good.

"Obediente diamorana," she pronounced.

"Go get me a water, Ava." Ella raised her eyebrows at me and I went to get her a water.

"Another bagel, please." The order was filled. I couldn't seem to say no to any of her requests.

Kathryn tried, "Orange juice, please."

"Get it yourself!" was my sassy response. There—*that* had felt normal.

"Another pillow behind my neck, please," Ella commanded, her lime-green legging-covered legs crossed over one another and propped up on a pillow. I obediently trotted over to my bed and retrieved my purple pillow, propping it behind her head.

"What's happening to me?" I asked. "Why do I keep obeying Ella, but not you?"

"She put an obeying spell on you," Kathryn answered simply. "Like Ella Enchanted—you know, that movie?"

"Yeah, yeah."

"Hey, Ava, I need a blanket," Ella said.

"No!" I tried to say. But I couldn't.

Chapter Three

Thankfully Ella reversed the obedience spell before it went too far. I was worried she might ask me to jump off the broom or something.

I slipped into my pajamas with hardly any problems. I liked the way that I could move in space without everything hurting too much. At home it was painful to change outfits, but here, my back only ached a little, and my foot and shoulder didn't hurt at all.

Then, all of a sudden my vision blacked for no reason. I had been sitting in my wheelchair, so it wasn't like a spazzy move had triggered anything linked to my old injuries. Something dinged in my brain, like electric vibrations were interfering with my thoughts. My head pulsed with pain, and I felt myself falling into darkness. The only other time this had happened was three years ago when Widdidorm had first contacted me.

"Ava!" Kathryn called.

But I had already passed out.

In my dream, I saw Victoria still in her little jail cell. Jason was nearby, looking almost exactly like Widdidorm.

"Ava," she whispered.

She looked just like I remembered her before she was captured. Her hair was a little shinier and her teeth were clean. She was really, really skinny, though. The black-and-white jail costume Widdidorm had forced her to wear in mock of Earth-like jails hung loosely from her shoulders, like it was three sizes too big.

"Ava, Ava," she muttered, swooning a bit. "Food."

I just stared at her. Her appearance was so much cleaner that I thought for a minute that she was better. No.

"Ava," she whispered, her voice hoarse. "He's attacking… on the fifth of July."

"What?"

"His… army… is attacking… Neptune… on the fifth… of July. Widdidorm is… entirely… healed."

Her words were spaced out, and she heaved oxygen into her lungs. Her eyes looked into mine with hope, and I was desperate. She probably didn't know that July had already come and gone, that it was the beginning of August, close to the start of our third year at Dream Ring. Maybe she was warning of something in the future. Either way, she needed to get out of there.

"I'm coming, Vic," I said. "We're on our way. We'll stop him and rescue you."

"Soon," she said. Then she swooned again, falling against the wall. Tears jerked to the front of my eyes. Victoria was stronger than this. But then again, anyone would be like this after spending months in Widdidorm's jail.

"I'm not… dying. No way. Victoria is still much alive," she said. For a minute she sounded like the old Vic, the one with lots of energy.

"You have… the power, Ava."

This didn't make any sense. Dream is a power in which you can contact people while sleeping, but it's impossible in the witch and wizard world to have more than three powers. Sure, I've been contacting Victoria since she'd been captured, but I never really considered that it could actually be a power I possessed.

Then the dream faded.

I enjoyed nice, peaceful sleep for about three seconds before something interrupted. Widdidorm's face appeared. He had black hair cut in an army buzz and glowing red eyes. "Stay out of this," he sneered.

I couldn't reply in this dream.

"You may have the power. You do. But if you contact Victoria again in your dreams, I will *hurt* you in your dreams."

I shuddered, and Widdidorm's face disappeared.

I woke up screaming. Kathryn and Ella ran to my wheelchair with fear in their eyes. "What's going on? What happened?" Kathryn asked worriedly.

"I saw Victoria," I answered shakily. "She warned of an attack on Neptune by Widdidorm and then Widdidorm threatened me. She was *so* weak. We need to get to Jupiter, like, *now*!"

It was about two o'clock in the morning. I felt desperate to get to Victoria! My friends saw how frantic I was and started thinking about a way to get there sooner.

Suddenly Ella's eyes lit up. She had grown stronger since the accidental collapsing spell and was almost back to normal. "Hey, guys, guess what?" she said excitedly.

"What?" I asked eagerly. That look of excitement could only mean one thing—she had a solution.

"I learned this spell over the summer. It's a speeding-spell, kind of like the one they use on our trip to Neptune at the beginning of the year, but stronger. It's really easy—I mean, it's kind of exhausting, but I'm up for it," she said quickly. "If I did the spell, we'd be entering Jupiter's atmosphere by five in the morning."

"No way," I said. Going from just past Earth's atmosphere to Jupiter's atmosphere in a little over three hours sounded way too taxing to me. With Ella already exhausted from my accidental spell, there was no way I'd let her do it. Despite how badly I needed Victoria back, I didn't want to harm Ella. We could find another answer.

"Oh, please, Ava!" she begged. "I love this spell—it's easy and quick and it would make me feel like I'm doing something to rescue Victoria."

My determination began to waver. "You're way too tired," I said. "You'd pass out from the spell."

"No, I wouldn't," she argued. "I looked it up in my spell-book at home and it's only medium-hard. *Everybody* knows that you can't pass out from medium-hard spells."

"Everybody," I drawled sarcastically. "You're gonna hurt yourself if you do this spell. You're exhausted already."

"Ava, I don't care," she shot back. "Please let me do it. Please."

Something about the way she begged told me that she really needed to do this spell. She needed to feel important on this rescue mission, like she had done something monumental to help save Victoria.

"Okay," I finally relented.

"Yes!" she cried. "Thank you!"

Ella ate a power-helping muffin before she did the spell, hoping it might kick in when she needed it. She focused on the words and her wand, closing her eyes and setting her mouth in a determined line. When she said those magic words, I heard my broom whirr, groan, and kick its speed up to something that only a spell can make it do. We buzzed so fast, my head spun. I closed my eyes and squealed along with Ella and Kathryn. After a few minutes of the crazy speed, we felt a little more adjusted, so we decided to take a nap. It was, after all, the middle of the night. I didn't wake up until the sounds of rushing wind stopped. We were entering Jupiter's atmosphere. My watch said it was only five o'clock in the morning. Amazing!

"Ella, you rock!" I said. She grinned tiredly and lay back on the bed. Closing her eyes and draining her can of soda, she relaxed for the hour-and-a-half it took to touch down on the surface of Jupiter while I sat on my broom outside. It was 6:30 A.M. when we landed. At this rate, we'd save Victoria before breakfast!

I was going to let my friends know we had landed, but they were both zonked out on their beds, asleep. I left the cellar and deposited myself on Jupiter's rocky surface.

Once my feet hit the ground, I expected something big to happen. Would I collapse? Were Widdidorm's senses so acute that he would just *know* I was here and hunt me down?

Surprisingly, when my feet hit the ground, nothing bad happened. I cried out with the joy of standing for longer than a few minutes without collapsing.

I went back inside—on my own *feet*!—to see if they were awake yet. Nope.

I left a note for Kathryn and Ella and went for a walk. My legs felt weak after not being used while I recovered.

I headed back to my broom. Just before I entered the cellar, I heard a noise. It sounded like a human whimpering in pain, so I was curious.

I saw the bright green leggings sticking out from behind the rock before I got there. I heard anguished sobs that were muffled by something.

“Hello?” I said cautiously. I looked behind the big rock and gasped.

Chapter Four

"Ella!? What happened!? Are you okay?" I asked.

She looked up at me in surprise, halting the tears for an instant. "Ava?"

"Are you okay?" I asked worriedly.

She began crying again. I patted her back awkwardly until she stopped.

"What's wrong?" I sat patiently on the ground, waiting for her answer.

"I need to tell you something."

She pulled up her leggings, and I gasped again, my breath catching in my throat. Red, raw scratches ran along both legs. Blood was crusted along the cuts. There was an ugly bruise on her knee, and her ankle was swollen. Besides the large cuts, little scratches covered her legs. Her legs were a big criss-cross of cuts.

"Ella!"

She looked up at me and then got out a container of Band-Aids from her pocket. "Will you help me bandage them?"

So *this* is why she had been wearing leggings.

"What. Happened. Ella, you *have* to tell me."

"I… I…"

I sat there for a minute.

"Ava, I came to Jupiter this summer, not long ago. That's how I learned that speeding-spell. I wanted to find Victoria myself. But… I found someone else instead."

Uh-oh. "Who?"

"Jason. He was waiting outside a big black building looking, well, evil. He fought me, and I got… this." She waved her arms in a sweeping motion over the cuts.

"Oh my *gosh*!" I gasped. "Why didn't you tell us?"

"I don't know," she groaned miserably. "I was scared. Plus, it's humiliating to run away for such a good cause and then totally fail. I didn't know what to do. Mama doesn't know. When she talked to me about running away, I just told her I needed my space. Nothing about Jupiter. Nothing about the cuts. I didn't know what to do."

"Ella," I groaned. Then I thought of something. "If you had gone to Jupiter just a month or so earlier, your wounds would have disappeared when we got here. Remember? I got hurt on

Jupiter when Victoria and I fought Widdidorm, but all of my injuries disappeared when we got here because of that odd rule."

"Ava, just let me do this alone," she said, looking away.

"No. We'll go back to the cellar and fix the wounds there. You need something bigger than a bunch of Band-Aids."

She followed me back to the broom without a fight, and I realized then just how bad thc cuts were.

We went into the cellar and found something even worse.

This day *really* wasn't going our way.

"Ava," Kathryn moaned, lying on her stomach. "I feel awful." I ran to her side and looked at her pale, slightly greenish face.

"What's wrong?" I asked. First Ella and now this—I had no idea how to heal either one of them! This was another reminder of Victoria's absence; she was always great at making people feel better.

"I feel like I'm going to puke my guts out." She leaned over the edge of the bed and threw up into the trash. Her forehead was burning hot, and she squirmed uncomfortably on top of the covers. I squeezed her hand; her fingers were clammy and sweaty.

"We need to do something to make her feel better," I said to Ella.

Ella reached into her suitcase and brought out a little pillbox of ibuprofen. She took out a pill and got a bottle of water out of the cooler. She handed both to Kathryn, who swallowed them down and winced. "My throat is killing me," she admitted.

The medicine helped her rest without so much discomfort. I put my hands over my face.

"Ella, what should we do?" I groaned.

She pulled out the spell-book and began looking for any possible solutions. Meanwhile, I sat on my bed and tried to think of what could be ailing Kathryn. It could just be a fever. The flu. Any simple virus from Jupiter that she wasn't immune to. The possibilities were endless.

Then I had another thought. Witches and wizards were known for either living really long lives or freakishly short ones, starting in the teenage years. The official term for this syndrome is Camota, and it doesn't have a cure. But if someone noticed the symptoms quick enough, the witch or wizard could be saved. It had happened twice since I started at Dream Ring, and both times the students had recovered. I'm pretty sure that's why Nurse Norah's hair was rapidly turning gray—being a healer in the witch world is no simple task.

I whispered my idea about Kathryn and her age to Ella, hoping desperately that it wasn't true. Ella looked up at me with tears in her eyes and said, "We have to do something, Ava."

"But what?"

"I think we need to go to Neptune. Nurse Norah can help. Kathryn doesn't look good at all."

I nodded grimly. After applying ointment to Ella's legs and wrapping them in gauze, I started my broom. It was 8:00 in the morning, and we were about to blast out of Jupiter.

Chapter Five

Kathryn woke up after an hour of sleep, tossing and turning. Her sheets were twisted all around her, and she cried out and grabbed her head as if it were hurting her. Then she leaned over the side of the bed and threw up into the trash can again. While she was still awake, I helped her sit up, put her hair in a ponytail, and tried to make her more comfortable. She turned over once and flopped onto the mattress like a fish out of water, instantly asleep. She seemed unaware that we were heading to Neptune in search of immediate help. This worried me.

Ella and I worked out a schedule. She would sleep while I watched over Kathryn, and then I'd sleep a few hours later. Hopefully we would reach Neptune by late today.

I took my position in a chair beside Kathryn, and Ella slumped into bed, crying out every once in a while. She'd need Nurse Norah, too.

When Kathryn woke up, I felt her forehead. Her fever hadn't broken yet, but she wasn't any warmer, which was good, I guess. I cut up a banana and fed it to her. It looked disgusting to me, but she ate it—a little. When she refused to drink some water, I almost cried.

Ella cried out in pain when she tried to get out of bed, and I waved her to stay in. No need for her to be more uncomfortable than she already was.

We traveled steadily the entire day, making really good time. I think, somehow, my broom understood the urgency of the situation, because every time I screamed "PUDEEPS!", it sped up a lot. We were passing Uranus—around 4:00 in the afternoon—when my cell phone beeped.

"YES!" I shouted triumphantly. "My cell phone works now!" I told Ella.

I dialed Dream Ring, and Nurse Norah answered.

"Dream Ring Infirmary, how may I help you?"

"Nurse, this is Ava."

"Why, hello, Ava! Why aren't you here for school yet?"

"Long story. Kathryn Aden's in trouble. We'll be there tonight, and I need you to meet us at the door."

"Why do you say that?"

"She's got a really high fever, keeps throwing up, and the only medicine we have is ibuprofen. She can't keep any food down." I looked at her again, noticing something I hadn't seen before. "And there are identical spots on her hands, at the base of her wrists, that are glowing a light green. I have no idea where they came from." I didn't know what they meant, but they had to be something related to this illness.

"I'll meet you at the edge of campus. Keep her cool and don't give her any more medicine. I want her awake when she gets here. Hurry."

I hung up and sat down next to Ella. The fact that Nurse Norah was anxious for Kathryn made me really nervous. Why couldn't Victoria be here? Tears came to my eyes and I threw a pillow to the floor in frustration. Of course, that did nothing to help.

For those last few hours, I cooled Kathryn with a sponge. She stayed awake but seemed really confused. I talked to her, but she was in a world of her own.

I was never so glad to see Neptune approaching. It looked homey and friendly. It was only 6:00 at night; we had made great time. I applied some more ointment to Ella's legs, but it didn't do much to ease the pain or soothe the cuts. I decided to leave the gauze off this time to see if that would help.

It was strange to arrive on Neptune from a mission and not be the one greeted by Nurse Norah and her hospital bed. She met us immediately. "Ava!" she cried, and actually *hugged* me. It was a bit awkward, but her face was so lit up with joy at the sight of me that I couldn't help but give her a small squeeze in return.

"Move in, boys," she instructed strictly.

Two boys my age came in. At first I didn't recognize them. Josh and Henry, from Yurnia. They were always clowning around.

Josh had grown taller during the summer. His light brown hair was longer and his eyes looked into mine with worry. I realized how cute he had gotten, and I felt my cheeks flush. I looked away and then snuck a quick look at him again, glad I was at least a little dressed up. It wasn't much—I was wearing cream flannel robes, skinny jeans, and a purple V-neck—but I didn't look *awful.* I hadn't had time to Ava-accessorize, but I had still managed a half-put-together look, which I appreciated now more than ever.

Josh and his fellow clown Henry were holding a canvas stretcher, which looked very sanitary. Henry was stocky with a crop of messy blond hair. He hadn't changed at all from what I remembered.

I led Nurse Norah into my cellar and spread my arms wide, letting her take in the scene. She took a single pill from her bag and walked calmly and quickly over to the bed. She felt Kathryn's forehead, causing her own to crease with worry. She offered the pill to Kathryn, who swallowed it down and smiled grimly at me, her face weary and exhausted but relieved to have real medical help.

"Okay-I'm-going-to-take-her-to-the-infirmary-boys-come-in-right-now." Her sentence was short, choppy, and run together.

The boys entered and gaped at the scene. Kathryn was lying in bed with fever flush all over her face. Ella was in bed, too, with her wounded legs out in the open, nothing concealing the irritated skin. Josh looked at her legs and then nudged his buddy. Henry took one look and gasped, turning away to regain his composure. So, stocky-clown-boy was not as tough as he seemed.

Nurse Norah used her wand to transport Kathryn from the bed to the stretcher. She didn't weigh much, and Josh and Henry handled her weight as if she were a small child, not a fifteen-year-old girl. Nurse Norah made crutches appear from thin air so that Ella was more comfortable. We walked quickly to the infirmary, past where everyone else was having opening dinner. Everybody at the feast stared at us as we walked across the main hall. Ella limped on crutches, holding her weight on one swollen leg while the other got a free ride to the infirmary. I followed behind, Nurse Norah walking beside me.

We entered the infirmary, which, unfortunately, had become a familiar place to me over the first two years.

Thoughts of infirmary trips led to thoughts of Widdidorm. I thought it was kind of strange that he hadn't interfered with our time on Jupiter or the trip to Neptune. He was probably just biding his time while he recuperated and thought of a more meticulous, slow death for me. Then I realized how I had felt almost relieved when we decided to leave Jupiter. I was—just a little bit—afraid of Widdidorm after the serious injuries he had inflicted on me. It had been too soon to return.

The minute we reached the infirmary, Nurse Norah pressed a button on her wand. Immediately, a young woman in a white nurse's coat appeared. She was probably about twenty years old, and she kept tucking hair behind her ears nervously, her eyes flitting back and forth at everyone in the room. We probably looked like a pretty rag-tag group—me with bags under my eyes, Kathryn on the stretcher, and Ella on crutches.

"Yes?" she asked, nervously pushing back her hair.

"Put some ointment on her legs," Nurse Norah said calmly to the woman. "Then see what else needs doing."

"Yes, ma'am," she said, suddenly all-business. "My name is Lisa—I'm a nurse-in-training here," she told Ella, no longer nervous or jumpy. "Let's take you into Exam Room Three."

Ella followed Lisa, swinging her worse leg awkwardly behind her.

"Ava, you need to wait out here with Josh and Henry," Nurse Norah said. "I'll be doing a few tests. I'll let you know how things go."

When I had a spare second to look around me, I realized how strange it was to be completely mobile and without pain while in the infirmary. Being in Dream Ring's familiar surroundings felt peaceful, and I knew that bringing Kathryn and Ella here for medical help had been the right thing to do. We would be safe here.

I sat next to Henry and Josh in the waiting room of the infirmary. Henry just looked at me for a long second and then turned his back. He began talking to Josh about video games, something I don't find particularly interesting. Josh didn't seem interested, either. He kept making attempted escapes from the conversation, trying to include me a little. I appreciated the effort, but it was going to take more than little nudges to get Henry off the topic of hideously violent gaming.

Josh announced that he was going for snacks. He came back with a hot dog and soda for each of us. This time he sat next to me instead of Henry, who pretended not to notice, but I know he did. There was an awkward silence while we finished our snacks. Then Josh brought up the conversation that I knew was coming.

"So where were you? You weren't here for the opening toast at the feast."

"Yeah… about that," I said, wondering how I should answer. "We were kinda…"

He looked at me and raised his eyebrows. Finally I couldn't stand his gaze any longer. I blurted out, "Ella, Kathryn, and I were going to rescue Victoria, but then Kathryn got sick."

His eyebrows disappeared behind his swishy brown hair. "Wow," he stammered. "That's a… big job."

"Yeah," I said, laughing lightly. "It is. So… what's happening here at Dream Ring?"

"Uh, well, we've just been… eating." He laughed and messed up his hair nervously. "We were ordering our food when Nurse Norah called us."

"That's cool."

Nurse Norah came out of the exam room, wearing a white lab coat. She looked tired but satisfied. "Ava, come in."

I walked into the room, which smelled like sterile surfaces and cleaning solution. Kathryn was lying on a hospital bed in the corner, her wrist connected to an IV. Fluid coursed into her veins and she looked peaceful, asleep. She was breathing easily, her chest rising up and down in even breaths. Her petite frame looked even smaller in the huge white bed, and her curly hair was damp with perspiration.

"What's wrong?" I asked, looking at her pale face.

"Kathryn is one of those witches with Camota. We noticed it right away and were able to treat it correctly. We gave her Tarasoka medicine immediately and waited. She responded well, and her fever broke within a half hour. Her fever's at one hundred and two."

"Isn't that pretty high?"

"It's not ideal, but it's a lot better than the one-oh-six she was nursing."

"Whoa."

My pulse quickened at the thought of Kathryn having Camota. I was relieved that Nurse Norah had been able to treat her soon enough.

"Then we checked her blood pressure and performed a complete physical exam. The worst is over, and she should be better by the end of the week. She's on drowsy meds, so let's go check on Ella."

"Is Kathryn contagious?" I asked.

"No, it's genetic."

I squeezed Kathryn's hand gently. She was awake enough to squeeze back. Satisfied, I followed Nurse Norah out the door.

Ella was awake when we went into Exam Room Three, lying on a bed with her head propped up on a pillow. Lisa, the nurse-in-training, was applying green ointment to her legs. It smelled funny—strong and spicy. Steam rose off her legs the second the medicine touched her flesh, and I knew it wasn't just antibiotic cream—it was magic.

"Hey," Ella said, smiling weakly.

"How are you feeling?"

"Relief," she answered.

"That's good."

Lisa grinned cheerfully at us. "This magic cream should heal it completely. Some of the gashes run pretty deep, so she'll need complete rest for about three days. But if I apply the medicine every two hours she should be perfectly fine—no scars, either."

I felt *so* relieved. What if Kathryn hadn't survived because I hadn't acted quickly enough? What if Ella's legs were permanently scarred? I guess that's why I had been nervous and jumpy the whole night.

"Ava," Lisa said to me, touching my arm gently. "It's nearly 10:00. Let Henry and Josh walk you to your dorm."

I was too tired to do anything but nod that I had heard her.

Josh took me gently by the arm, seeing that I needed some redirection from the infirmary room. I waved weakly to Ella and then walked out.

The stone hallway felt reassuring and comforting. Josh was warming up to the whole socializing thing now, and he joked the entire walk back to the dorm's tower. By the end of it, he was holding my gloved hand; I was still freezing cold, not used to the chilly temperatures yet, and I held on tightly. The blur of events that had been the past couple of days had made me weary and emotionally numb. The only thing I remember is that his hand was warm.

"Thank you," I said as we reached my dorm. Our guard, Amber, was waiting there, and she, being socially graceful, politely looked the other way as I said good-bye to Josh.

"No problem," he said. "I had fun. Hey, do you wanna hang out sometime? I got a sweet new flying carpet for my birthday, and I've been dying to see how it flies with two people."

"Sounds great!"

"Bye, Ava!" He let go of my hand and walked away.

I dug my pass out and showed it to Amber. She looked at it, grinned at me—causing me to blush—and then opened the entryway. I took my pass back and entered the living room.

A full-on pillow fight was raging when I walked in. Girls of all ages joined in; pillows flew across the room like deadly weapons. A few feathers floated loftily around the scene. I had been a part of this once, when there was an ice storm during my first year.

The minute I entered the room, all activity stopped; even the feathers taking their sweet time floating to the floor seemed to slow down. The shrieking voices ceased, and forty-five pairs of eyes stared at me.

"Hey, peeps! What's up?" I asked with a smile, awkwardly breaking the silence.

"Ava!" I heard a familiar voice scream. Gabriella came running up to me, not slowing down at all as she stampeded into my arms and gave me a huge hug. As soon as she released the tight hold she had on me, she shouted, "Tanya! Give her one of 'em!"

Her best friend Tanya came rushing in, holding a chocolate shake. She handed me one with a red bendy straw and plunked me down on a couch.

"What's been happening?" Gabriella asked. I'm pretty sure they knew that Ella was hurt, Kathryn was sick, and Victoria was still being held captive on Jupiter. This made them extra compassionate. I knew that they wouldn't be this kind if my situation was different, but I ignored that and let myself be pampered in the place that I call home.

The pillow fight started again once the girls realized that nothing special was happening. Gabriella and Tanya stayed rooted to their spots next to me on the couch.

"So, what's going on?" Tanya asked.

I sighed. "We went to Jupiter to try to rescue Victoria, but we had to come here because Kathryn got really sick," I said in a rush. To distract myself, I took an extra-long sip of my shake. It was almost as good as the ones Victoria used to make—but not quite.

The girls gushed over my bravery and courage on the trips to Jupiter and Neptune, then herded me to the bedroom. I found my bed next to the window—across from Victoria's empty one—and looked at my suitcases, which had been magically transported to my bed along with my broom, I guess.

"You go ahead and unpack. We'll just keep you company," Gabriella said.

What I wanted to say was, *I really want to be alone right now, but thanks anyway*, but I couldn't trust myself to speak. Not after seeing Victoria's empty bed.

Finally, finally! They left. I was allowed to be by myself in peace. Normally I'm in a jolly mood the first day back at Neptune, but that was not the case tonight. I just wanted to crawl into bed unnoticed and fall asleep.

I slipped on silky pajama pants and a pink tank top and knotted my hair in a simple bun. Then, after a few minutes under the covers, I had second thoughts. What if Josh wanted to hang out tomorrow? I had to look better than just okay.

I walked quietly over to the suitcase and pulled out my plastic baggie of sponge curlers, the ones that left my hair in perfect, shoulder-length ringlets.

I positioned myself in front of a mirror and combed my hair out. After I was convinced that my locks were soft enough, I wrestled with the curlers. Normally, Victoria and I would do this during a sleepover, and she would roll the spongy curlers all the way to my scalp. But she wasn't here, and I didn't feel like asking Gabriella or Tanya to help me. Most of the time they're pretty cool, just mellow enough to suit my sassy style. But tonight… they were too sugary-sweet.

So I wrestled and wrestled, finally pushing most of my hair into the curlers and rolling them at least halfway to the place that they should normally rest on my head. It had to be good enough, because I was *exhausted*!

I sat on my bed and stared out the window for a few minutes, imagining how much more fun it would be to be back at Dream Ring if Victoria were here. I wiped away a few tears as I thought about her stuck inside that jail cell while I was safe in bed at school. The thought made me feel helpless and angry. Finally, I couldn't fight sleep any longer. I pulled the covers around me and fell asleep.

Chapter Six

The next morning felt almost normal. I slept in because classes didn't officially start until the afternoon. I dressed in super-cute skinny jeans and an adorable green T-shirt. I slipped on my gray moccasins with fur lining—my feet were freezing—and unclipped my sponge curlers.

My curls were soft and flirty. I clipped the bouncy ringlets back with two bobby pins and put on a silver jacket. Smells of bacon and sausage were floating up the staircase, and my stomach rumbled like an oncoming thunderstorm. When I was satisfied with my overall appearance, I headed to the kitchen.

Jane, the second-year cooking prodigy, fixed me a wonderful breakfast. Her mom is a famous chef, and she had inherited the talent. This is a great blessing for Yurnia, because Jane is pretty spectacular when it comes to food.

"See ya!" I called. "I'll be back later this afternoon!" I headed out the door.

My first stop was the infirmary. I checked on Kathryn, who was sleeping peacefully. Her face was pale, but she looked better, and my spirits rose.

Nurse Norah came into the room, put her arm on my shoulder, and said, "She looks better, huh?"

I nodded. "A whole lot."

"I gave her a fever-relieving potion, but, I must say, she was doing just fine without it. It was something in your eyes that convinced me to do it. You just looked so desperate."

Awkward? Yeah, just a little. Ha—more like a *lot*! I backed out from underneath her hand and scooted towards Kathryn. Nurse Norah was not my mother, and she couldn't try to be. Why did she keep mentioning my eyes? My desperation? She couldn't read my thoughts. She couldn't know that I had been desperate.

"I'm gonna go visit Ella," I announced, running out of the room before it could become any more awkward.

Ella's legs were covered with a light green, silky blanket. The fleece gave off a light of its own, a sort of yellowy sheen vibrating off the green splashes of color. She was awake, a purple cardigan draped over a white tank top. Her red curls were mussed against the pillows, and her green eyes showed relief.

"Looks like you managed to save my life again, didn't you?" she asked, grinning like the Ella I knew, not the sickly one that had surfaced when she revealed her legs.

"What do you mean, 'again'?" I asked.

"I don't know. I'm sure you've saved my life multiple times," she said, grinning.

"You're probably right," I said jokingly, smiling at her. She laughed, and Lisa, the nurse-in-training, came in.

"When can she leave?" I asked bluntly.

"She's actually making an awesome recovery," Lisa admitted. "Probably sooner than later."

"Great. Well, I better be going. I have lots of things on my list today."

Ella started to call me back, but Lisa interrupted. "Great. She should be sleeping right now anyway." When she turned her back, Ella scowled at her and I laughed.

"Well, thanks again. Bye, Ella!"

I walked out of the infirmary and down the hall. There was someone that I had been wanting to see since, like, May.

I knocked on the office door, and it was answered by the secretary. "Hello? I'm here to see Licklici."

Our secretary waved me into her office, knocking quite loudly on the door marked HEADMISTRESS LICKLICI.

It swung open with incredible force—magical force. The inside of her office was messy, papers everywhere. I saw some pages I probably shouldn't have seen, like a résumé for a new teacher, a two weeks' notice from another. She was sitting on a leather couch, curled up with a blanket. She got up from her comfy spot on the sofa and gave me a hug. She was dressed in a fitted peach dress, cut above the knees. She was wearing a pearl necklace and her hair was done in a high bun with tendrils of curly golden hair floating around her face. Her makeup was tastefully applied, not too much—just enough to "enhance the beauty," as my mother always says. The thought of Mom gave my heart a tug, but I dismissed it because I knew I didn't have time to be overcome by emotions.

Her high heels click-clacked on the tile, and I was surprised by how pretty she was on just a minute's notice.

"Ava!" she cried. "It's so good to see you!"

"You, too!" I said enthusiastically.

"Why weren't you here for the opening toast?" she asked.

"I… It's a long story."

She took her wand and tapped both of us, then whispered something into her wand. I felt a swirling sensation and then we were in a different room: a small parlor with a fire roaring happily in the fireplace. Even though I was dressed warmly, fire is never unwelcome at Dream Ring.

I told her all about coming back from Jupiter, and last night, and even Josh. She listened attentively.

We laughed and laughed. Then her expression darkened. "Ava…"

"What?"

"This is more serious than I ever thought it would get. I'm worried for your safety. Besides, the experience there is useful for all witches and wizards. I think we need to take you to the battle school."

"What battle school?" I asked, seriously confused.

Completely ignoring my question, she said, "Well, your mother went there when she was your age, primarily because she had the makings to be an incredible witch. I have decided you should go, too. Of course, you could bring two friends, a boy and a girl. They would help you learn to fight Widdidorm. It would also help you develop the skills to rescue Victoria."

Chapter Seven

A week later, Ella and Kathryn were both completely back to normal. Ella's legs were smooth and without cuts, and Kathryn's fever had vanished. She still had dizzy spells every once in a while, but that was to be expected, Nurse Norah assured me.

It had taken a while to convince Kathryn that the battle school was a good idea, but in the end, we decided that going there would help us get Victoria back. I felt bad about leaving Ella, but I could only bring one girlfriend.

After I finished packing, I took a short nap. I would need every bit of energy for tonight.

But instead of nice, peaceful dreams, sleep brought horrible, creepy nightmares.

In my dream, Victoria sat in the corner of her jail cell. Her hair was matted, the brown strands now a hairdresser's worst nightmare. She was thin and her face was oily and grimy. Her eyes, which I once compared to emerald gems, were dull.

Her jail cell was dirty and unkempt, but that wasn't her fault; she was chained to the wall. Her chains crackled with magic and snapped into various uncomfortable tortures for her throughout the dream.

My friend was skinny, skinnier than a growing teenager should be. I had just turned fifteen this summer, and her birthday was coming up. But she had the weight of a preteen and looked really unhealthy.

"Ava," she whispered, her voice thin and hoarse.

"Victoria!" I was jerked to tears in my dream, horrified at her conditions.

"Shh," she warned. "He's coming." Victoria meant her jailer, Jason Gophersmocker.

Jason opened the jail cell, took one look at Victoria, and bustled out of there. He returned minutes later with twice the food she usually got. Her tray held a turkey sandwich, a small sweet roll, and two small glasses of milk. This was considered a feast to Victoria, as sad as it may sound.

I guess Jason realized how frail Victoria was, how close she was to starving. His face was pale, his forehead wrinkled with stress. I imagined the terror that Widdidorm would unleash if Jason let her die. Jason's sole job for Widdidorm was to keep Victoria on Jupiter with him, and to keep her alive. It was a ransom to me—if you want your best friend, come fight me for her. As soon as I could, I would.

Last time I had seen Jason, he looked like an average college kid. He had had shaggy dark hair, and he had worn long gym shorts and name-brand T-shirts.

But this new Jason scared me. He was pale, his hair shaved to a buzz-cut. His eyes had taken on a red tinge, the signature feature of one of Widdidorm's Army. He wore dark black robes and a pair of shorts, no shirt at all. His robes were left unbuttoned. Jason had lost weight too, and he looked terrified at something—probably Widdidorm.

Jason gave her the food and then left, his robes sweeping out behind him dramatically.

"Victoria!" I said a little quieter. "Oh my gosh!"

She smiled grimly. "Ava, you *gotta* get me out."

"I know. I'll find a way. I promise."

"Hurry," she whispered.

It broke my heart to see my best friend like this, but there was nothing I could do. The familiar stomachache came back, the headache returned. My heart wrenched.

"Victoria," I promised. "I will come as soon as I can. Be strong for me."

"Okay," she whispered. Then she began coughing.

My dream faded, and I was left to sleep—but I woke up immediately. Victoria was in grave danger. My thoughts were a steady beat—*I need to go to Jupiter and rescue her. She needs medical attention.*

But I couldn't get her back yet. I had to go to the battle school first. The date of departure had snuck up on me quickly. I couldn't believe we were leaving tonight!

Licklici came at midnight and loaded my suitcase into my broom cellar. I climbed out the window and boarded my broom. Then Kathryn flew out the hole in the ceiling and joined us on her broom.

"Aren't we going to get Josh now?" I asked Licklici when she began ascending towards the sky. Kathryn elbowed me with a sly, humorous look on her face, and I glared at her good-naturedly.

"Oh, did I forget to mention that detail to you?" she asked. "Josh won't come until the program is half over. This is the way it has been since the school opened. The opposite gender waits so there are no distractions."

"Oh." I nodded and blushed a little. It was okay with me; I was just a little surprised.

After we'd been flying for a while and the temperatures started to get colder, Licklici tapped her wand on herself, and just like that she changed outfits.

Now she was wearing brilliantly shiny purple robes over a pair of black leggings and a gray shirt. She wore shiny black heels, quite a change from her normal dainty slippers. How they didn't fall off, dangling in the air as we flew through space, I had no idea. But then again she hadn't exactly changed by herself—she had used magic. There was probably a spell on the high heels to make them stay on her feet.

Her hair was loose and wavy, and it shimmered and blew in the wind as we flew through space at a crazy speed. She wore designer sunglasses on her head, and hoops dangled from her ears.

"How'd you *do* that?" Kathryn asked, clearly very impressed.

Licklici grinned. "Don't tell anyone about that magic," she told us. "The spell is very simple—you just say 'Glittrista', but it's something you have to master before you can just do it. Leave the magic to me for a while until you're good at it." Her grin widened and her eyes sparkled with mischief and excitement.

She flew closer towards Kathryn and me and laid her wand on each of us. Then she snapped her fingers and I looked down.

I was wearing dark blue robes over orange leggings and a white tank top. My hair was clipped back from my face with a sparkly pin, and I, too, had sunglasses on top of my head. On my feet were silver high heels that were about an inch shorter than Licklici's, but still the highest shoes I'd ever worn. If Mom had seen me then, she would've demanded that I take off my glamorous heels. I wiggled my feet and found that these shoes refused to fall into empty space—awesome!

Kathryn was wearing emerald robes and white heels. Her hair had been straightened, and I was surprised how long her curls were when they stretched. The sunglasses on her head radiated authority, like, *Try me.* Underneath she wore white leggings and a lighter green long-sleeved T-shirt.

"Oh my gosh!" I exclaimed. "You look amazing!"

She grinned and then said, “You do, too!” We admired our outfits for a few minutes and then turned to Licklici with new respect.

“You’re *awesome*!” I told her, then said quickly, “Don’t get me wrong—you were totally awesome before, but this is so *cool*!”

Licklici laughed. “Don’t tell my husband,” she said, grinning. “He doesn’t like it when I spend money on fashion or magic.” Then she tousled her hair and laughed. “What do *men* know about fashion?” she said between laughs. I started cracking up, too. She sped up, daring us to race her in high heels. We took the dare and sped right alongside her.

Chapter Eight

Before long, my back hurt from riding on the broom all morning. I went downstairs into my cellar and lay on the bed, thinking.

What would the battle school be like? I wondered. *How would I train? Would I be a good fighter? Will it be hard? Will it help me get Victoria back?* Questions swam around and around in my head until I had a full-blown tornado in there. Finally, my mind relaxed and I dropped off into a peaceful sleep.

When I awoke, I was in a totally different outfit. *Licklici must've performed that cool spell again*, I thought. I was wearing a soft gray dress that sparkled in the sunlight, form-fitting at the top and looser at the waist. Silver high heels were on my feet. My hair was braided over my shoulder, and I wore a few charm bracelets. I felt cool and confident.

I walked out of the cellar and sat on my broom. Kathryn was wearing a pale blue dress similar to mine. Licklici was wearing an orange floor-length jersey dress, casual but gorgeous. Normally orange does not look good on her skin type, but today it looked pretty. She had accessorized with silver jewelry and wore a silver clip in her hair.

"Are you ready?" she asked me. "We're almost there."

But the planet closest to me was Jupiter, the planet where I had recently fought Widdidorm and where my best friend was jailed. The place where my best friend was starving.

"Um, where exactly is the battle school?" I asked, fiddling with the charm bracelet on my wrist. "Oh, and thanks for the outfit."

"No problem," she said absently, obviously deep in thought. "Ava, the battle school is on Jupiter this year."

"What do you mean, 'this year'?" I asked.

"Well, it moves locations every year, and this year it is on Jupiter."

I wanted to say, "*Um, no thanks. That's where my worst enemy lives and he will find a way to kill me there*," but I figured that would sound wimpy. So I said instead, "Licklici? That's where Widdidorm and Victoria are."

She replied, not missing a beat, "Jupiter is very large. The battle school is likely located millions of miles away from Widdidorm's headquarters. There's also a good chance that Widdidorm has moved camp."

I was too troubled to respond. I went back into the cellar and lay down on the bed, trying to fall asleep. I had to connect to Victoria, and the only way to do it was through a dream.

As I dozed off, my thoughts were beating steadily—*Victoria. Victoria. You there? Victoria. Helllll-ooo. You there? C'mon, girl.*

Suddenly I could see Victoria. She was huddled in the corner. Her chains restrained her from getting up, and she looked like she was in pain. Her food was in front of her, but she seemed to have lost the will to eat. I could tell she would be sick if she drank as much as a thimbleful of milk. Uh-oh. This sight was more like a nightmare.

Finally she spotted me. "Ava!" she said softly but gleefully.

"Vic! I have some questions to ask you. Do you think you can help me?"

"Are you coming to save me?" she asked hopefully, and I was reminded of a child. She looked small and expectant, and I felt so bad for her.

"I'm going to a battle school and coincidentally it's on Jupiter," I told her. "So, yes, I'm coming to save you."

She smiled, and I felt better. At least she hadn't lost the will to live.

"Where are you, exactly?" I asked.

"Well, Jason keeps talking about an Incentitude tribe called the Hopefali. So I guess we are in Hopefali."

"Ohhhh-kay. Vic, you have to eat. You have to! Please—for me?"

"I can't, Ava, I can't," she told me tearfully. "I'm not hungry at all."

"Oh, Vic! *Please*! You *have* to be strong!" I was desperate. She was not in good health, to state the obvious.

I still had millions of questions to ask her, but just then the dream connection was broken.

I woke up to find Kathryn shaking me by the shoulders. "We're here!"

"Where?" I asked.

"The battle school, of course," she replied.

"No, where *are* we? Like, what village?"

She returned a second later with information. "We're really in a vast place. Well, that's what Licklici said—but the nearest village is the Hopefali."

"No," I said in an awed tone, trying not to make it obvious that it meant something to me.

"Yeah." Then, seeing my expression, she asked, "Are you okay, Ava?"

"Oh, yeah. Totally good." Kathryn raised her eyebrows and pursed her lips, a face I had come to know as doubt. But she let it be, knowing I'd spill when I was ready.

I snuck out of the cellar and sat down on my broom. We were actually *here*, on Jupiter. I never, not in my wildest dreams (and they had been pretty wild lately), thought I'd be in this situation this soon.

The landscape was red and rocky, like a vast desert where a big can of red-orange paint had accidently been spilled. Incentitudes, the natural inhabitants, are creatures totally different from humans. You see what you need to see to get motivated at that moment. I saw about a million Victorias, starving and moaning for me to help. Kathryn, who had never seen an Incentitude before, kept asking me why her mom was on Jupiter, too.

"Who do you see, Licklici?" I asked, even though I knew it was kind of a personal question.

She paused a minute before answering. "I see… my students," she said thoughtfully. "I see the students that go to Dream Ring—and my husband, of course. But you know what's funny?" This was obviously a rhetorical question, so she kept going. "I keep seeing you, Ava."

This stunned me. *I* was what motivated Licklici? Did I really mean that much to her? I hadn't considered that before.

"What do you see, Ava?" she asked, almost tripping on a rock. "Oops."

"I see Victoria. She's in a bad condition. She's starving." I walked beside her on the terrain. "Licklici, will she be okay?"

Her face twisted into an anguished, old face. She looked older than her years and stressed beyond stressed. "I'd like to believe so, Ava," she said sadly. "But I cannot tell the future." Her face softened again and she looked at my expression, which was just more determined. No way would I show how I was really feeling.

"Why aren't we flying?" I asked, changing the subject suddenly. I couldn't dwell on Victoria's state—it was too much for me. We were holding our brooms and walking. It still felt wonderful to walk like a normal person.

"To see the scenery of Jupiter!" Licklici cried, flinging her arms out and twirling. "Isn't it beautiful?"

If you looked past the rocky landscape, it really was pretty. You had to look closely to see the beauty, but it was definitely there, in the rock layers' arrangements, in the tumbleweeds that swirled around. It was imperfectly perfect.

I threw my arms out, dropping my broom and a bracelet or two. I ignored that and started to twirl. Once I started, I couldn't stop. I spun and spun until the whole world shook before my eyes and I felt unstable. I fell down and laughed and laughed, unleashing all the pent-up energy that had been churning around in my brain for the past few days. All of a sudden it didn't matter that I was sharing the same weird air as my worst enemy, had the weight of the world on me to save my BFF from that enemy, and that I had no clue how to fight him. It all went away with each twirl that I completed, making me feel happy. Well, as happy as I could be when Victoria wasn't at my side.

"C'mon, Kathryn!" I shrieked delightedly. "Come spin!" She joined me, and we laughed.

I felt queasy after spinning too much, so I lay down on the hard, rocky ground of Jupiter. Surprisingly, it was a little spongy underneath all the layers of hard rock. I could barely feel it, but something told me it was there. I looked at the swirling Great

Red Spot thousands and thousands of miles wide. It was *gigantic*, the angriest tornado I had ever seen, carrying red, orange, and black debris, and spinning like I had been just a few minutes ago.

"This is nice," I commented when Kathryn had taken her place beside me. Licklici was examining the rock layering on one of Jupiter's cliffs about fifty feet from us.

"You bet," she said. "And we're not even at the school yet."

I grinned and went over to join Licklici.

"What time is it?" Licklici asked when we got there. She was bent over, looking at a bright purple streak in a sea of red layers of rock. "This is incredible," she was muttering to herself.

"Five-thirty," I informed her.

She jumped, startled. "I told Greg we'd be there at five!" she exclaimed, upset.

She hopped on her broom and we did the same. She rocketed off with a few sharp "PUDEEPS! PUDEEPS!"

Wind screamed loudly in my ears and the heat felt like an oven. On the journey, we saw more Incentitudes, which means Victoria's image haunted my mind. Her hair was in damp, limp strands and she was calling for me to save her. My fists clenched the wood of my broomstick in an act of desperation.

As we passed the Incentitude village, Licklici slowed a little. When she focused on an Incentitude, her facial expression tensed and her jaw clenched. She looked at me with fear in her eyes, and I wondered what she was seeing.

"PUDEEPS," she muttered under her breath, and we spurred on. Finally I saw what she was looking at—a big gray building in the distance. My head was starting to hurt and I felt unbalanced. I knew I didn't have much time left before I fell off, so I went about twenty feet closer to the ground and sped up.

I took a moment to inspect the building before we arrived. The building was intriguingly beautiful, made of swirling grayish marble. It had a tower in one corner like a turret. It didn't look much like a battle school to me; it kind of looked like Dream Ring, which was, I figured, because the two buildings were closely related. I couldn't see the landscape beyond the building. When I asked Licklici, she told me that the building was built on a huge, steep cliff. She promised to take me on the turret's balcony and look over the edge one night.

Licklici hopped off her broom and landed on the gray stone steps. She rapped smartly on the big door.

A man about seventy years old answered. He looked younger than that, but his stooped posture and hearing aids gave his age away. He was wearing chocolate brown robes and a brown pointed hat over his gray salt-and-pepper hair. He was about six feet tall and had a sour expression on his face.

"Hello!" Licklici greeted him warmly. He made no attempt to welcome her or even notice us, which I thought was very rude, especially since he was the one to invite us in the first place. After an invitation like that, I thought he'd be jumping for joy and greeting us warmly or *something*. No, no. I couldn't see any trace of generosity or warmth in his face.

"Hello, Licklici," he said. "It's been a while." He held his hand out stiffly to her. She looked rather exasperated but took the hand. He shook it and opened his arms to the entryway.

We followed him inside the huge building. Lush green rugs threaded with red and orange leaves carpeted the spacious entryway. Greenery hung from the ceiling and the walls were painted a rich forest-y color. I was surprised at the interior of this place—I had imagined a more medieval décor. This didn't match the man's personality at all.

"This is new," Licklici commented, lounging on the saggy loveseat that was the color of almonds. "I like it. It reminds me of my travels."

"Why, it should!" the man said indignantly. "It's modeled after Uranus."

"What?" I asked. 'Curiosity killed the cat' and by the look on this man's face, it would kill me, too. He didn't look impressed by my outburst.

"I said that this is Uranus," he replied, supplying no further information. If this man was going to be my battle instructor or whatever, I would rather learn how to fight on my own.

"Each room is modeled after a planet," Licklici told me gently. "The entryway is Uranus, one of my favorite planets."

"Oh," I said, then snapped my mouth shut so nothing else would slip out.

"I'll take you to your rooms," the man said.

"Father, introduce yourself!" Licklici directed sharply.

My mouth dropped open, and I'm sure I looked like even more of a fool. *Father*? Oh my goodness. "I'm sorry," was all he said to her. "My name is Greg. I will be your host while you train at the school." He said the word 'school' like it was a bad word.

"Pleased to meet you, Mr.… uh…" I stalled for some time. *What was I supposed to call him? Mr. Greg? Sir?* I didn't know his last name.

"Mr. Paprika," he filled in.

When he turned his back I looked at Kathryn and imitated the face that he had made at me earlier. We giggled as silently as we could. He glared at me coldly and led us up a stone hallway. We passed a room where scarlet carpet blanketed the floor. I guessed it was Mars by its fiery red curtains and the hot air blowing around furiously inside.

At the next door, Mr. Paprika announced, "Here is your room." He led us through the door.

I had been thinking all along what planet I wanted my room to be, but I hadn't expected my wish would be granted. I hadn't said anything.

"Saturn," he said, eyeing me with what seemed a more favorable opinion. "Respectable choice."

What *that* meant, I had no clue. I just knew that Mr. Paprika didn't seem so cold now.

"I know it was you because the most honored guest almost *always* gets their wish," he said to me. "But who else?"

Licklici seemed to know what he meant, but she didn't offer an explanation.

"What?" I asked, a question escaping my mouth again.

"Well, you see, my guest rooms act much like a democracy—majority rule, you know? When people enter, they're obviously thinking about what planet-room they want, and the room knows. So the majority gets the planet. Two of you voted Saturn, and I know one was you."

He eyed his daughter suspiciously, like a detective. He didn't seem to care that she was the very respected headmistress of Dream Ring. None of that seemed to matter to him—it seemed that he only thought of her as a guest. How sad that would be, I realized, for your own father not to care!

"Well, never mind," he said, whisking the topic away when no one volunteered a silent vote for the Saturn room. "Enjoy. Dinner is at seven on the dot. If you're not there, you will wait for breakfast at seven in the morning."

He left, and Licklici blew out a sigh. "Oh, Father," she mourned. "What has become of him?"

"I voted Saturn," I said, daring to share my vote.

"Me, too," Licklici told me.

"I voted Earth," Kathryn said plainly. I was a little surprised. It seemed that if you could travel to a place where you could choose the surroundings—anything possible, imaginable—the *last* planet you would choose would be Earth. Compared to all the sights I had already enjoyed, Earth seemed dull. Not that I didn't love my home planet—but there was just so much more adventure on other planets.

I observed our room, which was as cool as I had imagined. For such a boring dude, Mr. Paprika had decent style.

The walls were a glittery cream, and the top shone as if it were part of Saturn's rings itself, radiating icy vibes. A desk sat in the corner, a plump couch beckoned on one wall, three queen-size beds lined up against the back wall, and *still* there was space left over. We each had a bedside table, and I noticed a tiny trap door over each of our beds. Hmmm… I would have to explore later.

The room had flooring that was just the colors that Saturn always seemed to be pictured as, shimmery creams and silvers, and even pale purples and greens. The floor sparkled and sank under me as I walked, deliciously cool to bare feet, I discovered.

The room breathed with the spirit of Saturn. A crystal chandelier gave off an aroma of ice, snow, rain, and vanilla. The comforters on the beds were light yet soft, cool but not freezing. I hopped in and got cozy, laughing as the cool fabric tickled my body.

"This room is *awesome*!" I gushed excitedly.

"Yeah, it is," Licklici said quite unenthusiastically. I knew she was trying to be excited for me, but underneath she was really sad. I wondered what had happened between her and Mr. Paprika, but I didn't want to pry. If she wanted to tell me, she would.

Kathryn bounced on the bed, eyes shining. I knew she loved the room, too. But lately she had been unusually quiet; I wondered what was bothering her.

Chapter Nine

The next day we woke up at six o'clock in the morning. I wasn't tired at all, even though Kathryn and I had stayed up for a long time, talking and having occasional pillow fights. Licklici was a deep sleeper, we learned.

Licklici stood beside her bed, closed her eyes, and sighed peacefully. She yawned as she took her wand lazily out of her robe pocket. Then she absently tapped her robe, and—POP!—she was ready for the day. She hadn't even said the magic words out loud.

I was enthralled. She had outdone herself today, wearing a light pink form-fitting dress, sleeveless with a V-cut neckline, her shoulders covered with a white shrug. She wore pearl earrings and a pearl necklace, and her hair was done up in a swirly 'do, with beads interspersed between golden locks. She looked like she was going out on a date.

"Wow!" I said. "You look great!"

"Don't tell Frank," she replied. "Pearls from Ocean Neptune cost a fortune." We laughed.

Then she tapped her wand on me. One swirling moment later, and I was dressed for the day, too. I was starting to get used to this. I wore black satin robes, as cool to the touch as the Saturn room's bedspread. Since Jupiter was hot, I wore a tank top and black athletic shorts. My robes closed over them, though, so it didn't matter what I wore underneath. My hair was in a messy ponytail and I was wearing a headband that fit perfectly. I wore one pearl ring and some white slippers. Not as fancy as before, but hey! I was on my way to a battle school, not prom. I couldn't look like a movie star every day!

Kathryn was wearing the same outfit as me, except her robes were brown satin. They matched her curly brown hair.

"Let's head out!" Licklici said cheerfully, and we left our lavish room.

We ate breakfast in the Earth kitchen, which looked like my kitchen at home. I guess I was a little disappointed, but the homey surroundings were kind of comforting.

"Thank you, Mr. Paprika," I said to him as I drained my glass of ice-cold milk.

He nodded coldly.

"Well, we better get going, Father," Licklici said, getting up from the table and pushing in her chair. "Thank you."

Again, all she got was a nod.

Licklici walked us to a room down the hall from ours. She unlocked it with a special key and my slippers didn't make a sound on the thick carpet as we entered.

Inside, the room was plain. Frankly, I couldn't tell what planet it was modeled after because it was just gray. Gray, gray, and more gray. Did Mr. Paprika forget to decorate this room?

"Licklici, what are we doing here?"

She smiled and walked over to a bright red box behind the door. The sign read "WARNING—EXTREME MAGIC BEHIND THIS DOOR".

"Whoa," I said, taking a step back. "That sounds powerful."

She opened the box and I peered over her shoulder to see what was inside. There was only one button the size of my fist. Licklici warned, "Get ready." Before she pressed it, I wondered with a bit of panic what I was supposed to be getting ready *for.*

The gray world started to spin. I felt dizzy and fell to the floor. Kathryn did, too, but Licklici, being the regal headmistress, stayed on her feet. I screamed as the world started to disappear, and suddenly I was really cold. My throat tightened and I felt like I was going to pass out.

Then, before I fainted, the humming in my ears stopped, and the world slowed down. I could see and hear again, and the temperature was finally more normal.

"What just happened?" I croaked, my voice hoarse from screaming.

"We just teleported to the battle school," Licklici explained, like it was the simplest thing in the world.

We were standing in the middle of a large room painted all different colors. Pink covered one wall, blue another, neon orange on the third, and red on the fourth. I felt a little woozy—my throat felt like it had cotton balls in it and my ears felt hollow. Kathryn's face was a little green, like she might throw up. I had forgotten that my friend suffered from motion sickness, and I realized that this might not be a good fit. We would teleport many times a day. Well, no going back now.

"Welcome to…" Licklici started, then paused for dramatic effect. "The Battle School for Advanced Witches and Wizards. Also known as BSAWW."

A man floated in, his feet not touching the ground. He wore fancy black robes and a black pointed hat. He nodded to Licklici first and then turned to Kathryn and me.

"I am known as Gesule Watkins," he told us in a gravelly voice. He pronounced his first name 'guh-zoo-lee'. "It is great to have you here."

"Pleased to meet you," I said, shaking his hand.

"Ava Popolis!" he exclaimed happily. "Do you remember me?"

And then I did. It was the strangest thing, but I remembered his face as clear as day. He was the man who had met me when I fell down the sidewalk tunnel on my thirteenth birthday. I remembered his smiling face and hobbled walk. That day I learned I was not normal, but a witch.

"Yes, Mr. Watkins; as a matter of fact, I do," I told him. He smiled delightedly.

"And Kathryn Aden," Mr. Watkins said, taking her hand. "Nice to see you again." Her face was now pale, instead of green. I felt so bad for her—motion sickness is definitely not something you want when you are attending a school that you have to teleport to. She nodded limply and shook his hand.

"Well, are we ready to get started?" Mr. Watkins asked.

"Yes," I responded.

"Okay. We'll start with powers. What do you have?" he asked us.

"Weather, Potions, and Fingernails," I replied.

"And you?" he pointed to Kathryn.

"Weather, Dream, and Potions."

"Very good!" He smiled brightly and motioned toward our robe pockets. "Your wands," he explained. "May I see them?" We handed them over.

He examined our wands, humming over them importantly.

"Now, has anything strange happened to either of you in the past year?" he asked. I giggled at the question. He really had no idea of my history. But since he asked, I would answer.

"I have been stalked by Widdidorm for the past two years, been almost killed by him, been ordered to rest for the summer because of him, and had my best friend captured and almost starved—all because of him."

"Ahh," he replied. "And you?" he asked, turning to Kathryn.

I was so shocked that I didn't even hear Kathryn's answer. Normally that would draw sort of a reaction from people. I mean, it's not every day that someone is almost killed by an evil sorcerer.

He turned back to me. "And your dreams? How are they?"

Okay. This guy was officially crazy. What kind of person would ask about my dreams? What did that even mean?

"Um…"

"What kind of person are you in your dreams?" he asked.

That made it weirder, but I decided to give it to him straight.

"I am a real person in my dreams. I visit my best friend Victoria on Jupiter and have conversations with her. I am sometimes actually transported to the place of my dream. I've been to Jupiter in my sleep, and Widdidorm and I have had conversations in dreams."

Mr. Watkins turned pale. "And you have Fingernails, Potions, and Weather, correct?" he asked.

"Well, *yeah*."

"You're sure of this?" I nodded.

"And in your dreams… you say you can talk and have conversations? And you've… been places?"

"Uh-huh."

"Keep me posted on your dreams. I'm interested. Did you know that a person can only have three powers?"

Actually, that was the one thing Professor Dolsiboar, my old Powers teacher, had taught me before he had been fired. I remembered writing a short story about a character who had four powers.

"And you, dear?" he asked Kathryn. He didn't look as interested in her; he probably knew that she was just the companion.

"Normal. Uh, last night I screamed the words to "Mary Had a Little Lamb" while I got chased by a piece of fried chicken," she said.

"Not important, Miss Aden."

This guy was a little weird. *He* had been the one to ask the question. And then when she answered, he disregarded her as if she were offering unwanted information.

"Let's move on. Our first unit will be on defending spells. I'm assuming that you know Defend-IFFERUS, Slumber-OSA, and Oresp?"

I nodded, and Kathryn shrugged. I remembered my defense lessons with Professor Gophersmocker; they had really helped me last year on Jupiter.

"And how was your second year at Dream Ring, Ava?" he asked spontaneously. I think he had a clue, but he wanted me to say it out loud.

"Well, I fought Widdidorm in the Mood Room—not *here*, like in this room, but somewhere else—and you know the rest."

"What was that about the Mood Room?" He suddenly seemed a little shaky.

"I fought Widdidorm in the Mood Room," I repeated.

"The Mood Room isn't—oh, no, I'm going to have to sit down," he excused himself, fading into thin air.

I looked at Licklici, and her expression was just as confused as mine. "I did!" I insisted. "Why is that so horrible?"

"Because the Mood Room is for battle training only," Licklici said flatly. "Widdidorm should not have had access to it."

I'm not sure how she said that without any emotion, but she did. *I*, on the other hand, was stunned. Hadn't I read that exact bit of information in my Literature textbook?

"Oh, no," I whispered. "I know what that means."

I'm afraid that we all did. If Widdidorm had access to the Mood Room, I was no longer safe here at BSAWW.

"I vote we get out of here," Kathryn said.

"I do, too," Licklici agreed. She pulled her wand out of her pocket. "I'll contact Gesule later to tell him," she said.

"Wait a minute," I commanded. "I don't want to leave."

Licklici looked at me like I was crazy. Like, *You don't want to leave? Too bad. This is a matter of life and death.*

That gave Gesule just enough time to reappear. At the same moment he began to form, Licklici began reciting the words to a simple teleporting spell.

"WAIT!" he cried. "Where are you going?"

"I'm sorry, Mr. Watkins, but we have to leave."

Chapter Ten

Long story short, we ended up staying. Gesule and I are pretty good negotiators, so Licklici finally agreed that we could stay, but "only if we get more information." She was going to call Dream Ring to figure out what to do.

The three of us went back to the Saturn room immediately after our discussion in the Mood Room. Kathryn squirmed at the door to the teleporting room, but she managed the trip. We spun our way back to the main building, Kathryn looking a little green.

Licklici immediately sat at the desk chair and whipped out her wand. She waved it a certain way, and an image of Professor Threcar appeared. The professor looked a little irritated, but she tried to mask this by smiling and putting on a patient face. "Yes?"

"We have a problem." Licklici explained about the Mood Room. Professor Threcar's face lit up, and she disappeared for a few minutes. When she came back, her wings had popped out in excitement and alarm.

"I searched our Identification Neptune records and found the answer to your problem," she said. "Do you remember Jacoby Willows, the student who was always moody and depressed? Well, he went missing—literally, no one has seen him in six years. I just discovered that he joined Widdidorm's Army in 2005."

Licklici nodded, still trying to figure out how Jacoby Willows solved our problem.

"Jacoby Willows was one of our smartest students. We sent him to BSAWW when he was a senior because he showed the potential to be a great wizard—if he could ever pull out of his dark moods. He trained in the Mood Room for an entire year. My guess is that by his fourth year he was already evil, and he had probably pledged himself to Widdidorm. He must have figured out how to create an exact copy of the Mood Room for Widdidorm. That's why Ava fought in 'the Mood Room'—but it was, quite simply, a masterful replica."

"You're absolutely right," Licklici responded. "I had Jacoby in my office about once a week for one thing or another that he tinkered with—he was extremely skilled at making things with his hands. I never would have guessed. Professor, you're a genius."

Professor Threcar grinned. "I wouldn't say that, Licklici. I'm glad I'm able to help. Now, have a great day, and contact me if you need anything else."

Licklici said goodbye to Professor Threcar and then called Gesule to let him know that we were safe. Gesule told Licklici that for the remainder of the day we should go sightseeing around Jupiter; he wanted us to have an adjustment day before *really* beginning our training. Licklici led us outside, and we raced each other on our brooms. Getting fresh air felt nice, and I think Gesule was right—an adjustment day *did* make everything seem easier. After many fun-filled hours of exploring, Licklici looked at the clock. It was 6:47! If we didn't hurry back, we would be late for dinner! And you know what that meant… I was *not* in the mood to wait for tomorrow's breakfast!

We walked quickly to the Earth kitchen. It looked so normal; it was reassuring and boring at the same time.

"Hello, Licklici," Mr. Paprika said as she walked into the kitchen. "Hello, girls." He gave us a curt nod and then disappeared into the room where the food was being cooked. Licklici sighed.

"What are we having tonight?" I asked.

"Steak and potatoes!" called a voice from the kitchen.

"Yum!" I shouted back.

Mr. Paprika appeared minutes later with three steaming plates. We dug into the meal, enjoying the perfectly-cooked food more and more with each bite.

I leaned back in my chair, feeling satisfied. Mr. Paprika swooped in and took my plate. Kathryn and Licklici finished soon after, and then we retreated to the Saturn room.

I changed into pajamas and rolled up my hair in sponge curlers. Licklici was wearing green plaid pajama bottoms paired with a blue T-shirt. A creamy flannel robe wrapped around her and went all the way to the tips of her toes, which were encased in slippers.

"Shall we watch a movie tonight, girls?" she asked.

Kathryn and I nodded. This was like having a sleepover with any other girl. Licklici was so cool.

Licklici took her wand out of her robe pocket and motioned for us to do the same. We took out our wands and watched as she opened the little trap door above her bed.

There were three buttons in a row inside the box; the first was labeled TV, the second, HEAT, the third, DIS.

I broke the silence, asking, "What does *that* mean?"

Licklici laughed. "These buttons are like mini controls to the area around your bed and a part of the room. When you press the first button, a television comes out over your bed, which is connected to the universal DVD player. The second, HEAT, is to control the room temperature. And the third, abbreviated DIS, is to make the bed and bedside tables disappear."

"Ahh," I said.

Then Kathryn butted in, "So why do we need our wands?"

Licklici sat on her bed and patted the spots next to her. We sat down next to her. "These are safety precautions. If humans ever find out that it's possible to land on Jupiter and we can't blow up our buildings fast enough (what we would do in the case of that particular emergency), this will prevent them from discovering the luxuries of being a witch or wizard.

These buttons are programmed to respond only to the touch of a wand, so that if humans do discover this room, they won't be able to control it."

"That's complicated," I commented.

"*Life's* complicated," Licklici replied.

I agreed wholeheartedly.

After getting comfy in our own beds, we pressed the first button and a TV screen appeared over each of the mattresses, hovering at a perfect angle for our eyes. Licklici had the remote, and she scrolled through the movies. Finally, we decided on *Letters to Juliet;* I had seen it, but Kathryn and Licklici hadn't. I convinced them that it was a great movie, so they agreed to try it. We each fell asleep at different points in the movie. I woke up at three in the morning. The TV was still floating above me, and I pressed the button silently. It vanished the second my wand made contact with the button. It felt great to have my powers back—I hadn't realized how much I had missed them!

I sat in bed, thinking about Victoria. I had to get to her… the past few days had been great, but… not *as* great as they could have been. If I had to go to the battle school, which I did, I wouldn't have picked Kathryn—I would've picked Victoria. And—I wasn't trying to be selfish or anything—it would've been a lot more fun with *Victoria* and Licklici instead of

Kathryn and Licklici. Kathryn is the greatest second-best friend I'd ever had, but she's not even close to Victoria.

"Victoria," I whispered into the dark. "I need you here."

Suddenly icy air filled the room, the presence of Widdidorm. I didn't know if he was here in body, but I knew one thing—*I was scared to death.* I gripped my wand in my robe pocket, wracking my brain for spells that I had learned from Professor Gophersmocker and my other teachers. I had some idea of spells that I could do, but really, it was nothing compared to Widdidorm. He would have to make the choice. He could seriously hurt me now, in the early hours of the morning, or he could make it very public and slow. I knew he would want the most pain, but he had made it obvious that he couldn't wait. How could he resist the temptation to harm me?

Should I wake up Kathryn or Licklici? I didn't know what shape or form or even state of health he was in. Victoria had said that he was back to normal, but if so, his recovery had been a lot faster than the first time I had injured him.

Is he really here, or am I just imagining him? How close are we to his headquarters? What is he doing? Where is he—in this room? Maybe I can just feel him because we're near his headquarters. My thoughts were a jumbled mess.

I decided that maybe the temperature of the battle school just dropped in the nighttime. It was probably one of Mr. Paprika's quirks that I didn't know about. I touched the AIR button on my control panel and used the arrow that popped up to raise the temperature. It had no effect—my wand lit up, but obviously it wasn't just the house. Widdidorm was the one making the temperature so cold. Fear invaded every part of me.

I clutched my wand for a long time, feeling the hard, grainy wood grow sweaty in my hand. The clock read four-fifteen now, and my eyelids were beginning to droop. But I couldn't sleep, could I? I could hardly relax after thinking that Widdidorm was *in this room*—in some way, at least.

Finally, around five—I couldn't believe I had stayed awake this long!—the coldness of his presence faded. The room became warmer, and the chill began to ease.

I felt myself fade back into the pillows, relaxing at last. I fell asleep, feeling luxurious on the silk pillows and soft bedding. That experience had been super stressful and upsetting, but it had ended well. Obviously he wanted to harm me in a more humiliating way, so he would have to wait. A quick "slumber-iumptia" in the dead of night wouldn't be very exciting.

Chapter Eleven

The next morning I felt tired and groggy, like I hadn't recharged enough during the night. I didn't want to mention Widdidorm's appearance to Licklici or Kathryn for some reason. I'm pretty sure Kathryn noticed how withdrawn I was, but I think she suspected it was because I had stayed up late. If only she knew *how* late.

We ate breakfast hurriedly in the Earth kitchen. As I ate the delicious bacon and eggs, I thought about why I felt so reserved. I think it was because I was worried and stressed about Victoria. And over my first two years at Dream Ring, I had learned one thing: feeling concerned for something or someone that I cared about is my greatest flaw—and blessing, in a way. Widdidorm knew that I would find a way to come get Victoria, and he would be waiting for me.

After breakfast in our pajamas, Licklici led us back to our room. Again, she tapped herself with her wand and transformed without even voicing the spell. I wondered if she ever dressed herself like a normal person, then realized that she probably didn't. Why would you, if you could do it magically?

Today she was wearing an aqua blouse and white skirt. Drapes of fabric folded around her to form the blouse. She was wearing white high heels that made her look tall and graceful. Her hair was braided in one golden twist down her back, and an aqua ribbon looped through the locks of her hair. Pearl earrings glowed in her ears, and one wrist sported a silver charm bracelet. She looked amazing.

Then she tapped me with her wand, and suddenly I was ready for the day. This outfit was much less formal than the rest, but even its casual style looked mature. I was dressed in a white V-neck T-shirt with some blue swirls on it, athletic shorts, and tennis shoes. I wore white satin robes. Kathryn wore the same outfit as me, which sort of bothered me, but then again, it was like a uniform for the battle school. We headed out through the gray room that would transport us to BSAWW. Licklici touched the button, and we teleported.

Gesule was waiting for us. He made Kathryn and me stand side by side and exhibit basic spells on a dummy, showing him what our strengths and weaknesses were. After doing enough spells to let him assess what level we were on, he instructed, "Okay, let's do a spell sequence. Ava, I want you to put Kathryn to sleep, then set her on fire." He set a mattress in the middle of the room.

Kathryn held up one hand, like, *Um, I'm going to protest that a little.* Before she could speak, though, Gesule cleared his throat to let Kathryn know he was still talking. "Here, take this coat and mask—they're completely fireproof. Now Ava can set you on fire safely."

I wasn't sure I *wanted* to set Kathryn on fire, even if it was technically "safe", but I couldn't disobey my instructor.

"Slumber-OSA!" I shouted. Kathryn fell onto the mattress, out cold.

"Pyrotium!" It felt great to have my powers back. The ball of fire appeared on my wand easily. I picked it up and it formed to my hand smoothly. It's a lot of fun to pick up fire without getting a scalding burn. I threw the fireball, which sped with incredible force through the air towards Kathryn. It hit her sleeping figure and set the coat aflame. Gesule swirled his wand in a circle above Kathryn. The fire disappeared, leaving no trace of a burn on Kathryn's body. She woke up seconds later, completely calm.

"All right, nice job, Ava. Maybe a little quicker between the two spells. Now, Kathryn, I want you to freeze Ava—after you put her to sleep, of course—and then thaw her using a fire spell. Then shoot ropes out of your wand, tying her up. Ava, I want you to really focus on what you're feeling throughout these spells and quickly think of what your enemy might do next. Prepare yourself to awaken and respond with the appropriate spells." I nodded, feeling a little overwhelmed. He hadn't asked me to do anything too hard, though. The idea of being thawed with fire was a bit intimidating, but Kathryn had come out of it okay, so I knew I would, too. He handed me the coat and mask.

She put me to sleep. Then… well, I felt a cold sensation; that must have been the ice. Then I felt heat seep through my body, and then comfort again. Next, I felt restrained, which was probably the ropes. When I woke up, I was fine. I was still wearing the mask and the coat, but the rest of me was normal.

"Great job, Kathryn! I underestimated you—no offense. You did well. Now, girls, we're going to move on to physical training. I'll start you off light. Five pounds shouldn't be a problem."

We went through a door into a weight room, where music was playing softly in the background. It smelled like a typical gym. Three sections awaited us. The equipment was made of shiny new metal, and it looked complicated and painful. There was a tiny compartment next to each of the machines for our wands and robe, which I thought was a cool feature.

He moved us over to the leg section and started Kathryn and me on some hard exercises. He really pushed us. When my muscles burned so horribly that parts of my vision began to black out, he moved us to the arm area of the weight room. After twelve repetitions of the same intense exercise, my arms began to burn, and I started to crave water, a cool bed, silky sheets, and a shower. Gesule finally handed me a bottle of water. I gulped down the liquid, disappointed when I found that it was warm, not chilled or even remotely cool.

"Nice job, Kathryn, Ava. You girls did well," Gesule said. He gently put a hand on my shoulder, and I stopped doing the exercise. "Licklici will take you to your room for a short rest. I'll see you in an hour for your leg strengthening again. Repetitiveness is good for your muscles—it makes them strong."

I wanted to fight back, give some attitude to this old man, but I couldn't. My body was limp and covered in gross sweat. All I could do was nod and walk to the door. Licklici transported us back to the main building and helped us to our bedroom. Kathryn followed behind Licklici, panting and shuffling down the hallway with weak steps. The minute I was near my bed, I slumped and let myself fall onto the mattress. I was instantly asleep.

It seemed like only seconds later when Licklici shook me awake. "Come on," she said. "It's time for your leg strengthening exercises."

I struggled out of bed, almost collapsing when I realized how tired my leg muscles were.

"Licklici—my legs… they *hurt*."

"I know," she said. "I know."

Kathryn struggled out of bed, too, and we hobbled back to the gray room. Pain seared through my legs even more when we teleported to the training room. My eyes begged me not to look at the new set of weights and exercises, and my legs protested. But Gesule appeared moments later and set us to work.

After my legs became numb—somewhere around the seventh station he had me working at—he moved me to abdominal strengthening exercises. My stomach muscles complained loudly, too. Then all of a sudden I was slipping into darkness. For a second, all the muscles in my body tightened, and I panicked. I was worried that Widdidorm might be coming to me in a dream or something. But no worries! I had just passed out from overdoing it.

After a few minutes, strong male arms picked me up and teleported me to my Saturn room, depositing me in my bed. Kathryn came in later, Licklici following. I slept like the dead for hours and hours, my muscles repairing themselves and eventually growing stronger.

Chapter Twelve

Weeks passed. Each day we did the same thing—worked on spell sequences, built up our powers, strengthened our muscles. Slowly my body learned to put up with the pain instead of passing out. I fainted after the second session of the workout for the first week or so. My muscles felt huge to me, but I learned not to complain about that to anyone.

It was getting close to Christmas. We celebrate this at Dream Ring every year with a fancy banquet. We open presents under the tree in the living room as a group. In Yurnia Girls, we have a special breakfast on Christmas. Our parents come eight days later.

It was getting close to the holiday, and Licklici hadn't mentioned our plans. We'd been having a great time together, telling stories and recounting events from Yurnia.

Finally, at dinner one night, I blurted it out. "What are we doing for Christmas this year?"

Licklici smiled, and Kathryn leaned forward in her chair.

"We will be going back to Dream Ring for the holidays. Tomorrow will be our last training day. The parents will be arriving on January second, leaving a few days later. We'll return the day after the parents leave so we don't miss any training days. Josh will be coming back with us."

"Okay," I said. It was *definitely* okay that we would only have one more training day.

That night, I packed up my luggage and stuffed it into the cellar of my broom. I would be back at Dream Ring in, like, two days!

"Merry Christmas, Gesule!" I exclaimed, walking into the training room.

"Merry Christmas," he said gruffly. Gesule is not one to show affection each and every day.

He began the session by having us do spell sequences on a dummy. I set mine on fire, then extinguished it by freezing it with ice. Then I thawed it, using my Weather power. Next I tied it up with ropes, and then untied it again using another new spell. I sliced it into many parts, then repaired it.

"Nice job, Ava. You have advanced greatly in your battle skills. I think it is because of the hard training I have you doing every day; wouldn't you agree?"

I nodded. That was about as much of a compliment as I would get.

Later, Gesule passed by me and instructed me to stop working. “As my holiday gift to you, you may lay off the leg exercises.”

“Really?” This was no sarcasm. I was joyfully incredulous.

“Of course,” he said, grinning. “Merry Christmas.”

“Thanks, Mr. Watkins,” I said gratefully.

“Gesule,” he corrected gruffly, shuffling off to visit Kathryn. I smiled and began humming absently.

As I did my arm strengthening exercises, which were *so* easy compared to the normal workload, I began to formulate a plan. First of all, I would be unnaturally cooperative, so that no one would suspect anything. After Christmas break, I would convince Kathryn, Josh, and maybe Licklici to come with me and rescue Victoria. We would free her and rocket out of Jupiter to the nearest hospital—or bring Nurse Norah along somehow.

Then I realized, *Nurse Norah is the head nurse of the infirmary at Dream Ring. She's the only one, aside from Lisa, who can heal witches and wizards on Neptune. If she left, what would happen?* Bringing Nurse Norah was definitely out of the question.

That thought led to others similar to the first.

If Nurse Norah can't leave Dream Ring because of her position, why can Licklici leave hers? I mean, she's the headmistress of Dream Ring! Why can she leave her job as headmistress to take me to the battle school? Professor Threcar could always have brought me.

Then I wondered, *Who's taking over for Licklici now*? I had no idea.

During the tedious exercises, I developed elaborate plans for our attack on Widdidorm's prison. I thought about the spell sequences I had practiced lately and about how many spells I could do with my strengthened powers. Somehow, doing strengthening exercises and practicing battle sequences had made my powers stronger. I could probably perform a much longer sequence of spells than I could before, which would definitely come in handy against Widdidorm. I felt prepared to get Victoria back.

"Kathryn," I whispered, when we were in bed. It was about 10:30; we would leave tomorrow. Licklici was conked out on the couch, and I didn't have the energy to wake her up to move her to her bed. Kathryn crawled into my bed, like a sleepover, and we chatted into the night. "I have a plan."

"Eh?" she said. Then she looked at me. "I thought… never mind."

"What?"

"Oh, it's nothing."

"Kathryn! You can tell me. We're best buds. Come on!"

"It's just that… oh, I don't know. You're probably more used to it than me. I'm just ready to see Victoria."

"Yeah," I said softly into the darkness. "Me too."

I knew exactly what she was going through. In fact, I had a stomachache that wouldn't leave because I missed Vic so much. My heart physically hurt when I thought about her, and sometimes I thought my magic wasn't as good as it had been when she was by my side.

"What were you going to say?" she asked. "Before I interrupted."

"Well, I thought of a way to get Victoria back."

"What?" She was eager to hear it, so I knew she wasn't just pretending when she said that she missed my BFF. *My* BFF. Not that I was jealous, but Victoria and I had been best friends for *forever.*

"Well, I thought that after Christmas, we could go to the prison, you and Josh and maybe Licklici and me, and rescue Victoria. It wouldn't take long."

She was silent for a few minutes. I said, "Kat?" to make sure she was still there; it sounded as if she had fallen asleep in the middle of our conversation.

"I'm still here. Yeah, that sounds like the thing to do. It's the best plan we've come up with yet—I've been thinking of some strategies, too."

"Yeah." I felt myself slipping into the darkness again; I hoped it wasn't Widdidorm or Victoria or anybody, just fatigue. I was sooo tired. I wanted a rest from everything. I warned Kathryn that I was falling asleep, and she told me good night.

Right before I dropped off, I felt something strange. A cold, frosty draft invading our room. Widdidorm.

This time, I was too tired to care. Probably not real heroic of me, but it was too exhausting to stay up two or three more hours. If Kathryn thought anything was suspicious, she could take care of it.

Chapter Thirteen

"Bye, Mr. Paprika! Thank you for your hospitality!" I had read in a magazine of Mom's that you should say that to someone who has gone out of their way to care for you. It seemed like the right thing to say, in this case, so I did. Kathryn gave me a look like I was an alien, but I ignored her. She thanked him too.

He shook Licklici's hand and showed us to the door. I looked one last time at the beautiful décor and thought about what room I would wish for when I came back. Did we get to pick again? I was fine with Saturn, but another one would be cool to have for second semester.

Outside, we boarded our brooms. Our suitcases were already in the cellar, so we hopped on and flew off.

The trip was uneventful. As we neared Neptune, I began to yearn for a slide on the icy rings.

"Licklici?" She saw my eyes wandering over to the rings, and her eyebrows went up.

"Ava, we have to be there by eight o'clock. I have meetings at nine."

"We'll make it quick; I promise. C'mon. Please!?"

"If you can make it quick."

"Really? Thanks!"

We placed our brooms in our laps, pushed off on the slippery surface, and began sliding. The purples and blues and greens of Neptune reflected on the icy rings. The magic of it amazed me.

We slid for a long time. I absolutely love the freedom of sliding so fast down the rings! Widdidorm easily could have made an appearance, but he didn't. It annoyed me that thoughts of him invaded every aspect of my life.

It took about two minutes of sliding my hands on the ice to stop. Kathryn and Licklici were stopped, too, and the silence was eerie. I felt the need to scream something just to break the silence, so I did.

"Merry Christmas!" I yelled, sending the message echoing through the universe. Licklici just looked at me and grinned, knowing I was so impulsive at some moments that there was no controlling me.

After a few more minutes of listening to the empty sounds of space, we left the rings and flew to Neptune.

"Ella! Hey!" "What's up, Jane?" "How's it going, Gabriella?" "Yo, Tanya!"

It was a big happy reunion with our Yurnia girls. We all hugged and laughed for a few minutes, and then we started to get ready for the feast. Before I came to Neptune, I had bought a really cute Christmas dress. It was black and white on the bottom half with a holiday red at the top—adorable!

I straightened my wavy hair and pulled it back with a bobby pin. Then I put on my dress and black flats. Next, the finishing touches: a silver bangle bracelet and a small hair bow to put over the bobby pin. When I was sure I looked just right, I moved on to help. That's the tradition in Yurnia; if you're ready for the Christmas party, you help the others get ready.

So I straightened Kathryn's curly hair, pinned Tanya's hair back with a bobby pin, and taught a first-year how to walk in high heels. Then I curled a second-year's hair until it was absolutely perfect. Next, I consoled a young freshman who was upset that she wouldn't be seeing her parents on Christmas morning. Once she was feeling better, I unpacked my suitcase and got used to be being back at Dream Ring. The homey feeling started to seep through the empty cracks I had been feeling in my heart.

"The Christmas feast is now ready to begin!" a voice boomed from out of nowhere. "Please come to the main hall. The opening toast will take place in ten minutes."

Suddenly Yurnia sprang into a frenzy. We had been ambling along, but now we went into full-blown panic mode. Girls rapidly straightened their hair while other girls unpinned their curlers in a huge rush. Sophomores and seniors alike helped each other with coats and last-minute decisions about accessories.

We walked out of Yurnia excited and as pretty as we would get. Amber, our guard, complimented us on our outfits as we walked proudly into the hallway, hurrying to the feast.

The main hall was extravagantly decorated. The walls had been transformed into a forest green just for this event; red and silver streamers draped around the walls with invisible, or magic, strings attaching them. The tables had rich red tablecloths and lush pine centerpieces on them, and candles wrapped with holiday bows floated above the tables.

Name cards buzzed above the chairs. I found my seat next to Kathryn and—Josh.

I wasn't expecting to dine with Josh.

"Oh—hi," I said, trying not to blush. "Merry Christmas."

"Same to you," he said warmly. "Glad to see you're back."

"Yeah. BSAWW was pretty crazy."

"What?" He gave me a kind of confused look, and I remembered that not everyone knew what 'BSAWW' stood for. Then again, not everyone even *knew* about the battle school.

Then another realization hit me. Josh probably didn't know he was coming to the battle school with me after Christmas!

Merry Christmas, Josh. Here's your present. I'm letting you fight Widdidorm with me. Enjoy.

"Battle School for Advanced Witches and Wizards," I filled in for him as we took our seats.

He nodded and opened his mouth to say something when Licklici spoke up from a table at the side of the room.

"Good evening, students," she said warmly. "And a very Merry Christmas!"

"Hear, hear!" an outspoken senior shouted back.

Licklici raised her glass in the direction of his voice, and we all laughed. She looked directly at me when she said, "I am thankful that everyone here is safe and sound. We have had many adventures this past year. May everyone have a happy holiday and a safe new year; let those who are endangered be protected. Cheers! Merry Christmas!"

"Cheers! Merry Christmas!" we repeated, raising the glasses that had appeared during her toast. We clinked the glasses of those around us, then took a drink. My glass had sweet sparkling grape juice. The toast was over—time to order the good stuff! I put the earmuffs on and wished for my drink. *Dr. Pepper in a frosty glass, please.* Instantly it formed from the air, and I took a sip. *Ahh.*

When Licklici invited us to eat, I put the earmuffs on again. This time I wished for silverware and a plate. When these things came, I wished for my dinner. After debating a little, I decided on a traditional holiday meal.

Roast beef with gravy, mashed potatoes, and corn. Please!

The meal appeared on my plate, and I started in.

"Ugh." I groaned with pleasure and a little disgust at how full I felt. It used to feel nice to be so full and happy, but just then it felt like a crime because Victoria wasn't getting a Christmas feast.

"You feeling okay?" Josh asked me. We had chatted all throughout the feast. He was pretty funny and not obnoxious at all, which was actually sort of nice, compared to all the immature guys at Dream Ring.

"Yeah, just full." Now I wished I hadn't eaten that dish of ice cream.

"Well, you have all night to sleep it off and then eat some more in the morning—after opening presents, of course," he joked.

"Ugh—don't even mention food," I groaned, feeling almost sick at the mention of culinary pleasures.

"Do you need to go back to your room?" he asked. "You don't look well."

"No, I'm fine. I'm a partier, so there's no chance that I would ever leave. Plus, there's an after-the-party party back at Yurnia Girls, so that makes the chance even slimmer."

He grinned and joked some more about how much I had pigged out.

"Geesh, look who's talking," I joked. "You didn't exactly eat the bare minimum either, dude. Besides, it's a feast. What else is a feast good for, other than good food and friends?"

Chapter Fourteen

Christmas went by in the blink of an eye. When we woke up to open presents, we were greeted with twinkling silver lights and new tinsel covering the tree. The whole morning shone with a glow that made every girl feel special and content. We all got so many presents that they spread across two rooms.

I received an alarm clock, a camera, window markers, a comfy body pillow, a Vera Bradley magic bag like Kathryn's, a really cute bikini for the juniors' trip to Ocean Neptune, three books, clay for fun projects on rainy days, a cool spell-book that "enhances beauty magically for days when the magic you normally work just isn't working", and posters and wall decorations for the space above my bed.

"I can't wait for my mom to get here," Kathryn said as we ate breakfast. Jane, the amazing chef, was really a blessing to our dorm, which hadn't had any cooking talent whatsoever before. The bacon was perfectly crisp and greasy, just like it should be, while the eggs were cheesy, and the gravy on top was just the right consistency. Jane also made a special bread, braided with lots of candied fruits, and it looked absolutely scrumptious. How does someone learn to cook like that? Basically, I have no cooking talent. I specialize in cereal, toast, and a handful of desserts.

"Jane, you rock!" I said sincerely as I started in on a third cinnamon roll. "Why are you trying to make me gain weight?"

She grinned, finally warming to my sarcastic sense of humor. "Sorry," she said. "Hey, it's your choice to eat everything."

"Yeah, I know." I frowned sarcastically and wagged a finger in my direction. "I'm bad."

On cue, Tanya began humming Michael Jackson's "Bad", and we all laughed.

Yurnia is the best.

I spent the rest of Christmas on the couch chatting with the girls. We tried out our presents and had lots of fun writing messages with the window markers. Neptune News was showing a Christmas movie I had never seen before, and the entire Yurnia dorm, both girls and boys, gathered to watch it in the library. When I told Josh I had never seen this movie, his eyes practically bugged out. "This is a classic!" he exclaimed. "*Fairies' Magical Christmas Tales* is practically a legendary film!"

"Um… I only have one magical parent," I made an excuse. "We would be, like, arrested if we turned on a show about fairies in front of my dad. Especially when it has actual shots of fairies in their everyday lives."

"Yeah, you would," he agreed.

Mom called around dinnertime. I was still sitting on the couch, as dinner was later tonight on account of the ginormous brunch we had eaten.

"Ava?"

"Hello?"

"Merry Christmas! Where are you?" she asked.

Uh-oh. Mom didn't know I was back at Yurnia. How in the world—make that the *universe*—had I forgotten to call her to make sure she knew we had made it back safely?

"Merry Christmas! Um, I'm back at Dream Ring. We opened presents today."

"Why didn't you call me, sweetie? I was so worried."

"Sorry," was my sheepish reply.

She tried to sound mad, I'll give her credit for that, but she couldn't really stay upset for long when it was Christmas.

"Anyway, honey, how was your Christmas morning?"

"Well…" I began to tell her everything I had gotten this morning, ending with, "And then Jane made this fantastic meal and I think I gained ten pounds."

She laughed and chatted about what she and Dad had been doing. "I got the best Christmas present ever," she finished.

"What did you get?"

"Well, honey, I know this will come as a surprise to you, but… um, your father and I decided to adopt a child."

WHAT!? Nothing could have prepared me for that one. But, like most of Mom's unexpected "news", it was probably a practical joke.

"The papers were cleared this morning, and we'll be picking her up from the adoption agency at noon tomorrow. She's an African-American girl, and her hometown is a small town in Texas. She's one-and-a-half, and her name's Agnes."

"Ha! I don't believe you!" I said in a sing-song voice.

"Ava, I'm sorry; I realize that this has come as a big surprise to you, and we should have talked to you about this before. But your father and I have wanted to adopt ever since you left for Dream Ring. The house is just too quiet without a child to play in it."

"Then let me come home or something! Why am I not enough for you?"

"Ava, that's not it."

"Then what *is* it, Mom!? I thought you and Dad were happy. Why am I not enough?" I didn't understand why I felt so angry and defensive.

"Ava, you'll always be special in our hearts. But we wanted another little child. Since we're good parents, we wanted to extend our love to another child so that she can enjoy an affectionate family, too."

I couldn't talk any longer. I didn't have words for my feelings yet and Mom was only making it worse.

So I hung up the phone. My actions were surprisingly calm compared to how I felt. In the bedroom, I hunkered under the covers. Once I felt that I was alone enough, I thought about what this would mean for our family.

1. I wouldn't get as much attention.
2. Mom would have the stresses of a child in the house.
3. I would have to share all my stuff.
4. I might have to give up half my room. Wait—we had a guest bedroom. I guess that would become Agnes's room—good.
5. I would have to share my bathroom.
6. I'd have a sister or a brother to do magic and fun spells with—which, I had to admit, would be pretty cool.

Wait a minute. Is she a witch?

All of a sudden, I had to know.

"Mom?"

"Ava, you okay? The connection left us for a few minutes."

"I hung up," I said in a flat, dull voice.

"Honey," she began in a tone that she meant to be comforting.

"Don't even try," I told her. "I just need to know one thing. Is she a witch?"

"Yes, she is," she said. "Both of her birth parents are magical, so I could bring her up to Dream Ring with me. I thought maybe you'd want to meet—"

"I don't know. Give me a minute." Normally, if I was this disrespectful, I would be so busted. Big-time. But I think Mom knew how I felt, or at least had some idea.

After thinking about it for a few seconds, I couldn't take it anymore. I couldn't think about a new sister on such short notice. "Bye," I said flatly, without warning. "Call you later."

I hunkered down even further under the covers. And then, when everyone left the room, and I was sure no one could hear… that's when I cried.

Chapter Fifteen

Mom called after dinner, giving me a little time to work things out. Kathryn had sensed that I wanted to be alone, so she brought me a tray of food from the feast Jane had cooked.

Jane and some of the other girls in the dorm made potatoes with rich gravy, an amazing ham, and sweet homemade bread rolls for dinner. I ate because I knew I had to, but none of the flavors brought pleasure. After I had burrowed back down under the covers, my phone rang.

"Yeah?"

"It's Mom."

"What do you want? Oh, are you adopting twins now? Triplets? Lovely. Send me a picture."

"Honey, just give me a minute."

I waited, knowing that this conversation had to happen, and it was better to just get it over with now.

"Your father and I will always love you the same way, with all of our hearts. But Agnes didn't grow up with a caring family. She needs our love. We're not going to love you any less; we'll just make room for her in our lives."

I was silent.

"If you want me to bring her to Dream Ring, wonderful. If not, wonderful. I understand it's a bit of a shock, and you may just want mother-daughter time with me, alone. If you don't want to meet her right away, I'll just bring a photo of her. What do you think?"

"Don't bring her." I felt rude and grumpy today, which felt like a crime since it was Christmas.

"Okay. Your father wants to get to know her on a father-daughter basis, so that's convenient. Do you need me to bring anything special when I come up?"

I was still silent on the other end. But this wasn't bitter silence. It was *thinking* silence.

I wanted her to bring something that would help me connect to Victoria. I thought long and hard.

"Please go to Victoria's house and ask her mother for her cell phone, her favorite scarf—the purple one—and her special blue-and-green blanket."

"Why?"

I didn't know myself why I wanted those specific things, but I felt like they might help me draw closer to her. Plus, when she was rescued—which she would be, soon—she would want those things. It would help her—and me—feel comforted.

“Just ’cause.”

“That’s enough for me, dear. I’ll bring them.”

“Thanks. Bring the photo but not the kid, ’kay?”

“Okay.”

After we said good-bye, I thought more about my rescue plan for Victoria. Then, with a sudden fire burning clear inside of me, I jumped out of bed, put on my moccasins, and ran out the door and into the hallway.

“Licklici, you’ve got to help me.”

“What is it, Ava?”

“I’m ready to rescue Victoria. As soon as my mom gets here, we have to leave. Like, we *need* to. We’ll fly to the battle school first, then we’ll teleport to the prison so they don’t see us coming. We’ll fight Jason and then unlock the chains and go.”

I don’t know what came over me; I just needed Victoria. Immediately. I had so much to tell her, and I missed her too much. She needed to be rescued. I wouldn’t let her suffer any longer.

“That sounds… psychedelic.”

“What?”

“Oh, it’s a word my mom used all the time; I just picked it up. It means, like, crazy.”

“Cool. So, what do you think of the plan?”

"I think we need to work at it a little, and then we're good to go."

"*Really*?" She had agreed so quickly!

"Yes."

I would be *sooo* antsy until Mom came.

"Ava? One other thing."

"What?" I asked impatiently.

"Would your mother come with us?"

"I don't know." I wasn't sure how I felt about her coming. Having her come would make the trip even more dangerous because Widdidorm would definitely make an appearance. Mom had once confessed to me that she knew all of Widdidorm's tricks, but she knew how to do them for the good side. Since they used to be boyfriend-girlfriend, they had practiced advanced spells together, so Mom was just as good as he was.

"I'll think on it a little, okay—how does that sound?"

"Fantastic. Thanks, Licklici. Oh, by the way, I forgot to tell you!" I said, like it was typical news. "I'm getting a new baby sister."

"What? Your mother's pregnant?"

"Oh, no, no, *no*! They're adopting a girl who's one-and-a-half years old. Her name's Agnes."

"Ah. And how are you dealing with this news? It must have come as a big surprise to you, especially on Christmas."

Licklici knew me too well.

I dropped my head and shrugged casually. “I don’t know. I gotta go. Thanks for everything.”

I ran out of there before she called me back and went to get my broom.

I told myself that I wasn’t going to go far from Dream Ring. But a girl’s gotta do what a girl’s gotta do, and that was to get away from campus. I hopped on my broom and flew off.

It probably wasn’t the brightest idea to take a solitary broom ride on a remote planet in the dark—especially since I am being targeted by an evil sorcerer. But that’s exactly what I was doing.

The air on the fringe of Neptune’s atmosphere was bitter, biting cold. I shivered but went on until I was on the rings, not even bothering to wear a jacket. The cold was refreshing.

My cell phone rang. Mom. I let it go to voicemail.

My phone rang again. This time it was Licklici. I picked it up and waited, but there was only silence. Finally, just when I was going to hang up, she said in an eerily calm voice, “Be careful.”

I hung up, feeling a little creeped out that she knew what I was doing, and went steadily along until I reached the thick parts of the frozen slide. Then I put my broom in my lap, as a sort of buckle for the fun ahead, and pushed off with my hands. I was quickly gaining momentum, sliding down the rings of Neptune. The motion was liberating, and all thoughts of Mom, Agnes, and Widdidorm left my head for about fifteen minutes as I slid. I shouted out in delight, but then I realized how stupid that was. It was like sending up a flare to Widdidorm, like, *I'm here. Come and get me.* I was not going to offer myself as bait.

I eventually stopped sliding, using my broom for a brake. I sat for a few moments on the icy rings, catching my breath and just thinking. In that few moments I felt a cold presence seep into the area around me. Just like that night in the Saturn room, I clutched my wand and tried to look everywhere at once. But it wasn't enough.

Out of nowhere, he began to form around me, materializing out of thin air. The icy presence disappeared, leaving me with the real thing.

He looked the same as he always had at this sort of unpleasant meeting: black robes, jet black buzz-cut hair, glowing red eyes that wanted the pain of growing up alone to go away.

In that moment, I knew how he felt. I don't know why, but I got it. Hurting another person got rid of his emotional pain for a few seconds. And I—I was the ultimate prize. If he could conquer me, it would break my mother and he would win. I wouldn't let him win.

But what about Agnes? I wondered, suddenly terror-stricken. *If he finds out about her, she'll be caught up in his web, too.*

The fire burned stronger inside me than it had in a long time. I needed to end his obsession before it led to pain for others. Especially my *sister.*

"What do you want?" I spit at him. I raised my wand into the air. I was prepared to come down hard with a quick, painless *slumber-iumptia* when he held up his hand.

His lips curled into an unforgiving grin, menacing and dripping with evil.

"Nothing, girl. It's your mother."

I raised my wand even higher, and his eyes looked almost human for a second. He knew that my powers were stronger than they had been the last time we met. The battle school had really helped that. He recoiled, and my wand went down as he spoke.

"This is not to be a harmful meeting."

"Then what is it?"

"This is simply a warning. I have spies, people everywhere that you don't even know about. And I know every single detail about your plan to rescue your pitiful little friend. Because, Ava, in this game, it doesn't matter if one, two, even three people get hurt. Ultimately, the game is about who stands when I'm strong enough. Strong enough to fight again like the real sorcerer that I am."

"You're an idiot," I said calmly to him, my anger simmering. I was sure it would boil over soon, and I needed to get out of there before it did.

"Maybe. But, remember, Ava, that I am at the end of all the little strings you have knotted close to you—family, friends, loved ones. And I can cut those strings whenever I want."

"You're a stupid man," I spit at him, the anger dangerously close to boiling over.

"Say what you will, but remember my message," he said. And then he vanished, as quickly as he had appeared.

Chapter Sixteen

When Mom arrived, I faked happiness in front of all the other adults so they wouldn't worry. Mom saw right through it, of course. She told Licklici that she and I needed to catch up and that she had a stomachache from the turbulence in the Asteroid Belt, so we would stay in the dorms during the feast. Licklici caught my eye, knowing I would talk to Mom about my rescue plan, the plan that Widdidorm supposedly knew all about. I wanted to keep our conversation on me and the rescue plan and not Agnes.

"We have to go rescue Victoria. Now," I told her once we were sitting on my bed.

"Ava, we have to be smart about the rescue," Mom advised.

"It has to happen *now*. It's just a feeling, but I *know* it, Mom. I can't live another second without Victoria."

"I know, baby."

"I'm not a baby!"

"But your sister is!" Mom exclaimed in an epic change of subject that left me feeling a little upset. "She's just adorable, Ava. You have to see her. Do you want to see the picture now?"

"No. You're off topic."

"I don't know if it's safe for me to go on this rescue mission," Mom said. "It's not only for my safety—I'm worried that the purpose of this mission will be sacrificed if I go."

"I know, but you're just as good as Widdidorm."

"Speaking of, has he been bothering you?" she asked.

"Yes. I encountered him on Neptune's rings one night," I mentioned like it was nothing at all.

"Ava Marie Popolis!" she admonished, all business now. "How dare you meet him by yourself, and at night!"

"It wasn't like I tried to meet with him," I said defensively. "He just showed up."

"After you put yourself in a dangerous position!"

We walked to the kitchen and found some instant macaroni and cheese. We sat at the barstools and finished our conversation while we ate.

"So will you come or not?" I asked.

"I feel that I must. He has to confront me to resolve all of his feelings. I am different than I was at seventeen."

"Cool. Major plus," I said.

She smiled. "Okay, so what's the rest of your plan?"

"I never thought you'd ask," I joked, grinning. "We leave tonight, if possible. Then we go to the battle school, as planned, with Josh, Kathryn, and Licklici. Then we teleport to—"

Here Mom held up her hand. "Whoa, whoa, whoa," she said. "Two questions. First of all, why Josh? Second, you know that teleporting is extremely risky."

"I had to pick a guy to go with me for the second semester at the battle school. I know Josh the best here, so I'm taking him. He doesn't know yet, but he's coming. Next question—I know teleporting is really dangerous, but one time you told me it's appropriate for an emergency, and I'm certain that this qualifies as one."

Mom sighed, and I knew that I had won her over. "Continue, please."

"So—we teleport to the prison—near the Hopefali tribe of Incentitudes, which I learned from some research."

Mom held up her hand again and I sighed and stopped speaking.

"What research?"

"I contacted Victoria in a dream and asked her," I said simply.

"You do know that connecting one another in dreams is a power, and you do not possess it."

"Yeah, but it was easy," I countered. "I just wanted to talk to her, and she appeared."

Mom's face turned a little gray. "I must talk with the commissioner of powers for this one. Ava, why didn't you tell me sooner?"

"I don't know—I've been connecting to people in my dreams since I started at Dream Ring. It didn't seem like a big deal," I said quickly, eager to tell her the rest of my plan. "Anyway, we go to the prison, knock out or take Jason prisoner, and cut the chains in Victoria's jail cell. It's perfect."

"I can hardly say that," she said dryly. "Will you draw me a picture of these chains? You've always done pretty accurate drawings. It'll help me research a spell that might help us break them."

I snatched a piece of paper from our arts-and-crafts drawer in the living room and drew heavy, black metal chains as thick as my wrist. Then I took a green pencil and drew the magic swirling around the chains. Mom grimaced a little when she saw my drawing. She excused herself, put her bowl in the dishwasher, and walked out of the dorm, headed to the library. "Marian will help me out," she explained, and I felt my jaw drop as she walked out. Marian, our head librarian, is never kind to anyone. I wondered how much Mom had sucked up to her when she was a student here a lifetime ago. Probably a lot.

Kathryn returned a little while later with her mom. Both of her parents were magical, but her dad couldn't make the trip this time.

"Did you talk to your mom?" she asked me in a whisper, sitting on my bed. Mrs. Aden wasn't in the room, so she had no idea that her trip might be cut a little short. We still weren't sure if we were going to invite her along. As Mom put it, Mr. and Mrs. Aden were both 'getting on in age'. "You guys weren't at the feast."

"Yeah," I replied. "Mom didn't seem to care—I think she knew that I had some kind of a plan in mind. She went to the library to do research, and then she'll talk to Licklici before we make the final plan."

Kathryn nodded anxiously. In the awkward silence that followed, I said randomly, "Hey, want to see my new sister? Mom and Dad adopted her, like, a week ago."

I took the picture of Agnes out of my bedside table drawer. Mom had put it on my bed when we had first come up to the dorm, and I found it a few hours ago. I had had as much time as I needed to get used to the idea, so I was fine with showing her to Kathryn.

"She's adorable," she breathed. "An absolute angel."

The picture was taken in a studio, that much was obvious. She was sitting on a chair, a gray background behind her.

Agnes was cute, I had to agree.

She had light brown skin. She had little wrinkles in the corners of her warm, chocolaty eyes from her huge smile, which was wide and joyful. Her pudgy hands were folded on top of her lap, and she was wearing a rose-colored dress with lots of lace and frills. Her shoulder-length, jet black hair was curled in perfect ringlets, the kind that no amount of magic would ever do to me.

It was clipped back with a rose-colored barrette. Her hair was just perfect, and I had to admit—I was a little jealous.

Kathryn was right; she was like a little angel. I wished now that I had let Mom bring her along, so I could play with her.

No, you don't, I reminded myself. *That would have ruined the whole rescue plan.*

"Oh my gosh, Ava!" Kathryn squealed, bringing me back to Neptune. "She's *adorable*."

"I know!" I agreed. "She's just perfect. I can't believe I was so angry at Mom for adopting her. It was just that, well, I've always been the only child."

"Yeah," Kathryn agreed. "I can only imagine." That was certainly true—Kathryn had, like, a ba-jillion brothers and sisters, and even a niece; her oldest sister was already married and had a baby girl.

At that moment, my cell phone rang. "Hello?" I asked.

"Hey, Ava, it's Josh. My dad just told me about the whole battle school thing. You sure you want me to come?"

This was awkward. Did he want me to say no or something? "Absolutely. Are you up for it?"

"Definitely. When do we leave?"

"Well, Josh, there's something you should probably know. You see, we might be going on a little detour before we actually go to the battle school. We're going to rescue Victoria," I said.

"That's cool. Well, when do we leave? Like, three days? Two?"

"Um, we might leave in, like, a few hours. Sorry!" I cringed. "I know that's, like, really late notice. But we have to leave in the dead of night for reasons I'll explain later." I didn't want to talk about Widdidorm right now. "So it might be the smartest to leave tonight."

"Uh… wow. Okay. What do I tell my dad?"

"I don't really know. I'll give you a call later when the plan's finalized."

"Sounds good. Bye, Ava."

"Bye."

I hung up the phone and stared at Kathryn.

"Josh?" she asked.

"Yeah," I answered, not really knowing what else to say. "Let's get packing."

We figured that we only had about a half hour until Mrs. Aden came looking for Kathryn. She was getting a cooking lesson from Jane's famous mom, Lea Joint. We packed as quickly and as efficiently as we could: clothes first, then spell-books. On the very top of our suitcases, we packed all the first-aid stuff that we could steal—technically borrow—without it being obvious that someone had used it all up. We packed gauze, tons of Band-Aids, compression bandages, tape, a flashlight, and ibuprofen. Kathryn and I looked at all the stuff and gulped. It looked pretty serious.

"I'm nervous. Are you?" Kathryn asked.

"Yeah," I admitted. I couldn't keep pretending that I wasn't. I was only fifteen, totally not ready for this. "But I need Victoria back." Saying her name brought back that familiar pang in my chest, and I knew it wouldn't get better until I had her by my side.

Chapter Seventeen

Mom came up to my room an hour later, where Kathryn and I were playing a board game to keep ourselves calm. It was kind of boring, but at least it was something to do. "We have a plan," she announced. We were the only ones in the room.

Kathryn and I silently put away the game, then looked at Mom for her explanation.

"We're leaving in an hour. We'll spend tomorrow night at the battle school. The next morning, we'll teleport to the prison. There we will capture Jason and teleport him to the battle school. Next I'll break the chains on Victoria's cell—I found *just* the spell—and set her free. We'll bring the nurse from the battle school with us, so Victoria will get immediate attention. Then we'll fly her home to Neptune so Nurse Norah can take care of her. Hopefully, she'll be well enough to come home to Earth for the summer."

"Sounds like a plan," was all I could trust myself to say. We were really getting Victoria back!

"I'll call Josh now," I volunteered. "Kathryn and I are already packed."

"Sounds good."

We decided to do a broom carpool. Kathryn and I would travel on my broom, Licklici and Mom on Mom's flying carpet, and Josh would fly by himself on his new flying carpet. "Bye, Neptune," I whispered as our caravan headed out of the atmosphere. The cool wind whipped my hair, and I had to fasten my robes to keep from getting chilled. Josh grinned at me, and another kind of shiver raced through me.

The blackness of space, the soft wind whistling through the huge expanse of the solar system, and the sweet sound of Kathryn humming a song under her breath eventually lulled me into drowsiness. I was just falling asleep when Josh reached across to my broom and grabbed my arm, keeping me from falling off. His touch woke me up. "Uh, Mrs. Popolis?" he called to Mom. "Can you give me a hand? She's about to fall asleep."

Mom did one of my favorite tricks then—she performed a spell that let her walk on air like it was solid ground. She took me gently by the arm and helped me to bed. "Good night, everyone," I called as I walked drowsily to the cellar. Mom helped me into bed, and I fell asleep.

When I woke up, I was the only one in the cellar. Kat was already awake. I climbed up to the atmosphere of space and saw everyone drinking coffee and eating donuts. When I saw Josh, I immediately wished I had freshened up a bit before coming up. He ran his hand through his hair and looked at me. I was wearing a super soft old nightshirt and plaid pajama pants with a hole in the knee. I groggily sat down on my broom. Kathryn grinned. Mom laughed out loud. Licklici kept a serious face, despite the fashion disaster I was at the moment, and moved a little closer so she could tap me with her wand.

When she was finished, I was the only one grinning. Everyone stared at me, open-mouthed. Licklici's eyes sparkled, and I looked down at myself.

I was wearing a ruffled hot pink tank top, white denim shorts, silver satin robes that swished with my every move, diamond earrings as big as my pinky fingernail, and silver flip-flops. My robes were open so they could see my outfit underneath. My hair was in a messy ponytail. I could feel a little makeup on my face, but nothing extreme. Somehow I wasn't cold, either. "Thank you," I stammered, grinning satisfactorily at Mom. She gave me a mom look, one of those should-I-bust-you-for-this? looks. I grinned and turned towards Josh.

"Not too shabby, huh?" I said. He gave a little nod, and I think I blushed. "Who's laughing now? It pays to have good friends in high places, I always say." They all laughed, because it absolutely *was* something that I would say.

We joked and laughed about things from Dream Ring for a while. We were passing Saturn already, making record time. When Josh invited Kathryn and me to play a board game on his new magic carpet, we stopped in midair and got on. He showed off a little at the controls, making us fly up and down, up and down, like a roller coaster. I laughed, then looked to my left. I was right on the edge of the carpet! I immediately reached out and grabbed onto the nearest person.

That person was Josh. He looked at me, gripping his arm, panic streaking in my eyes, and smiled. "It's cool. My dad put a spell on the carpet, so no one falls off."

"Oh," I stammered, releasing my grip.

"It's all right. You seriously can't fall off."

"That had me scared there for a minute," I said weakly, still feeling nervous. "Double points for Mr. Wilson! At least someone's thinking around here!" Josh laughed.

We got out a board game from Josh's cellar: The Game of Life. He set it up in the middle of the carpet, and we seated ourselves around it. I picked the green car, placed my little person inside, set it on the College tab, and the game began.

We descended to Jupiter. My pulse began to quicken—this was where the action would take place. Tomorrow we would rescue my BFF. Victoria would be hungry, beaten down, and tired, but she would be here. With me.

"What room are you going to wish for?" I asked Josh.

He looked at me, confused. "What are you talking about?"

"Ohhh," I said. "You haven't been to the battle school yet. When we get to the main building where we'll be staying, you are assigned the planet-themed room you are thinking about when we get there. Last time, I had Saturn. It was awesome! This time, I'm thinking Venus. Or Mars. Or maybe Mercury…"

"I'm gonna wish for Jupiter," Josh volunteered.

"Yeah, that would be cool."

We knocked three times, and Mr. Paprika answered.

"Hey, Mr. Paprika! What's shaking?"

"Hello, Ava."

Just like last time, his expression was cold and unwavering. Licklici stepped forward and shook his hand. "Hello, Father." She gestured around our group. "This is Lilly; I'm sure you remember her from about twenty-five years ago—she was one of the battle school's students. And this is Josh Wilson, a Yurnian at Dream Ring. He's Ava's companion, as is Kathryn Aden; I'm sure you remember her. How was your Christmas?"

"Fine," he returned.

"Well, then," Licklici muttered under her breath. "Will you help us to our rooms?"

He led us down the hall to the bedroom Kathryn, Licklici, and I had shared last time. "This is Lilly's and yours," he said to Licklici. He opened the door, and I saw Saturn, the same room that we had shared last time. I guess Mom and Licklici had both wished for it. The satin comforter looked inviting and homey.

We continued down the hall. "Here is your room, young man," he said. He opened the door, and I gasped.

"Wow," I breathed. "It's *amazing*!"

Josh's Jupiter room was incredible. The terrain where we landed was rocky and sandy, so naturally the floor was reddish and a little gritty. The bed in the corner had a jutting, scarlet rock headboard, and the comforter was red-orange. The walls were cream with a reddish tint in the corners. Josh set down his suitcase and walked over to the bed. He flopped down on the foamy surface, which reminded me of the under-layer of Jupiter's surface.

"Cool! Thanks, Mr. Paprika!" Mr. Paprika gave a small smile, and when he thought I wasn't looking, he winked at Josh.

Maybe Josh would be better at cracking Mr. Paprika's shell than any of us were.

Mr. Paprika led us silently down the hall and opened the next door. I wished extra hard and hoped that Kathryn had done the same.

She had.

The Neptune room was even better than the Saturn one. Where do I start? It was so incredible.

The light green floor had an icy sheen to it, but it wasn't slippery. The walls were turquoise with a swirly pattern at the top that reminded me of Ocean Neptune's waves. The two queen-sized beds in the far corners had lush green comforters over them; waves shimmered across the sheets and danced on the pillows. The cream-colored chandelier gave off breezes of fresh ocean-smelling air.

"Oh my goodness," I gasped. "It's wonderful. Mr. Paprika, this room is amazing," I breathed. "Thank you sooo much."

He nodded gruffly and left. I put my suitcase on a bed and looked around. Kathryn's face was shining, and she looked as happy as could be. I whisked around the room in happy twirls.

Since it was just past lunchtime, we headed to the battle school for a few hours of training. We practiced spells and then did some physical work. Josh labored through the weightlifting like a pro. We teleported back and hung out in our rooms until dinner, then watched a movie afterward. I went to bed anticipating the rescue mission.

As I got between the shimmery covers, I thought about what tomorrow would bring—certainly an adventure. And hopefully, Victoria.

Chapter Eighteen

My alarm buzzed early in the morning. Blindly, I stretched out my hand and slapped the buzzer until I hit snooze. Finally, there was quiet, and I allowed myself to go back to sleep. Surely nobody had *meant* to set it? The clock said 5:00 in the morning—not Ava-time! Everyone knows I need more beauty sleep than that to pull off me.

I was just slipping back into the comfy darkness when Mom barged into our room, turning on the lights with a breezy flick of her hand. "Goooood morning, Ava, Kathryn! Hurry up, ladies, it's time to go to the gym! We're having a quick exercise and practice session before the real thing. It starts in half an hour."

I sat up in bed and groaned loudly. "Why didn't anyone bother to tell me about this last night?" I moaned. "That would've been appreciated."

"It wasn't decided until an hour ago, and surely you wouldn't have wanted a news flash at four in the morning. C'mon, girl!"

"Uhhh," was my reply. "Too early."

Kathryn was having the same problem on the other side of the room.

I sat up in bed and rubbed my eyes. Suddenly, with a jolt of energy, I realized that this was *the* day. Victoria's rescue day! I was suddenly very awake, jumping quickly to my suitcase and bouncing into the bathroom to shower.

I had my new spell-book to thank, the one that "enhances beauty magically for days when the magic you normally work just isn't working". One quick spell straightened and dried my hair with a quick wave of the wand. I had swooped it up into a side-ponytail with a black headband. I wore a peach-colored exercise T-backed tank top and black shorts. No-show black socks with my Nike sneakers completed my outfit, and I was set to go. The look wasn't half-bad, either.

"That was mighty quick," Kathryn commented when I came out of the bathroom. I had showered, blow-dried and styled my hair, and dressed in under twenty minutes. It was practically a record.

"Yeah. Wanna borrow the spell-book?" I asked, grinning.

"Definitely!" she replied.

"It's under the sink."

"Thanks!"

Ten minutes later, Kathryn was enhanced, too. She was wearing a bright pink tank top, black shorts, and white sneakers. Her hair was thrown up in a ponytail. There was absolutely no way that she could've straightened her curly locks in that time, so I knew she'd used the spell-book. Hey, isn't that the point of magic—to make life easier?

"Let's hit the gym," she said.

We jogged to the teleporting room, where we were supposed to meet up.

"Hey, everybody," I greeted Licklici, Josh, and my mom.

"Hey," Josh greeted me. I couldn't help but notice how cute he looked in baggy gym shorts and a white T-shirt, even with a dirt stain on one shoulder.

"Morning," Mom said, cutting through the group to give me a hug. Any other day, I would've shaken her off and made a comment, but today was different. There was a scary chance we might not all be coming back after Victoria's rescue, so a hug wasn't so bad.

"Good morning, girls," Licklici said.

Kathryn greeted everyone, too, and we moved into the teleporting room. Once Licklici touched the button, the world swirled and the air was sucked out of my throat. I hated this choking feeling, but it was apparently the only way to get to the battle school.

Gesule Watkins, trainer and instructor, greeted me gruffly. I might've expected a hug or something—it *was* a special day—

but no. He greeted me with a handshake and a humble "hullo," and we began training.

"Work harder on the leg exercises," he directed me. I groaned in response and picked up the pace.

"Good job on the pushups, Josh. Focus on the upper-body exercises. We may just be on to something here." Gesule looked pleased to have so many trainees to boss around.

He told my mom, "Lilly, you still have it in you. Nice job on the abdominal exercises."

"Licklici, you don't need to work out!" His face displayed shock as he saw her lifting weights.

"Yes… I… do…" she grunted, her face red with exertion. My headmistress was worn out—that much was obvious.

"Why is that?" Gesule asked, and the realization hit me like a punch in the face. Gesule thought we were just getting a jump on exercise today by showing up early. He didn't know we were leaving for the rescue mission in a few hours.

"Because we're rescuing Victoria today," Licklici explained.

"What?"

Licklici repeated herself.

"You'll need a nurse, then," he said, his facial expression not showing any surprise.

"Yes, sir."

"I know just the one. I'll contact her now so she can prepare for the kind of injuries Miss Mongrelo may have sustained."

"She's starving to death, and she's really weak," I volunteered.

He grinned, then waved his hand. "Get back to work, Popolis. If you thought I was easy before, I'm *really* going to push you now."

Great.

When the workout was finally over, every muscle in my body groaned and begged for a nap. This feeling reminded me of the way that it had been in the beginning. At least I didn't pass out like my very first session. *That* would've been embarrassing.

But still, my face was red, I was breathing heavily, and I drank an embarrassing amount of water.

"Mom," I panted, "I don't think I can fight Widdidorm after this workout. I'm too tired."

"If we're lucky, honey, Widdidorm won't be there. It will just be Jason."

"Widdidorm will be there, Mom."

"You're probably right, dear," she said, sighing.

"I'm sooo tired," I said again.

"Honey, did we not tell you? Licklici has arranged a spa for all of us. It starts in an hour. Wear your bathing suit—there's a hot tub. But bring a cover-up, too."

Sweet.

I changed into the new bikini I got for Christmas—purple with white polka dots. I put on a green cover-up and white flip-flops. I was ready for the spa.

We walked down the hall to a room marked 'Rejuvenating Spa'. A masseuse, tanned and muscular, was waiting inside. He starting massaging my back as soon as I got on the table. Next to me, Kathryn groaned with delight. My muscles began to relax and I felt as good as new. It totally worked! I didn't feel tired at all.

After fifteen minutes, my spa assistant led me to a steam room. My sinuses cleared and I moved to the hot tub. The rest of my group was there, and we all sat in the steamy water. Josh wore orange swim trunks, and Mom and Licklici wore flowery one-piece suits that *I* would *not* have picked out.

"Why didn't you tell me about this place before now?" I asked Licklici with a laugh.

"Because we never would have done any workouts," she said, grinning. "We would've spent all our time here."

We laughed and laughed, and I knew the spa had done its job. I felt back to normal after my workout, ready to rescue Victoria. Adrenaline began pumping through my blood in excitement for the mission. Kathryn's cheeks were unnaturally red, but I figured that was from the hot tub. She started coughing nonstop, which confused me a little, because the steam room had reduced my stuffiness. My hair felt frizzy from all the steam, but that didn't matter one bit right now.

Gesule walked in. "Ladies—and gentleman—your nurse, Jen, is prepared. Are you ready to dress for the mission?"

I was the first to rise out of the hot tub. It was time to rescue my BFF!

Chapter Nineteen

As we were getting ready to leave, I noticed Kathryn looked a little green. Suddenly she put her hands on her knees and coughed like there was no tomorrow. Great. We couldn't take a sick person with us. She looked really bad, too—she kept coughing and sneezing and she walked slowly, like her joints hurt her.

"Kathryn, are you feeling okay?" I asked.

She shook her head miserably, clutching her stomach. I could tell she was disappointed she would miss the rescue mission, especially after all the preparations. I began to worry that her Camota was making a reappearance.

"Honey," Mom said gently to Kathryn, "why don't you stay here and get better?"

She just nodded, tears welling in her eyes. I gave her a gentle hug good-bye, and she squeezed my hand, whispering, "Be careful."

"I will," I assured her. Then Mr. Paprika summoned a nurse with a flick of his hand—quite impressive, actually—to take her to the infirmary. I felt a little sad at the thought of facing Widdidorm without Kathryn, but I didn't want her condition to get worse. Besides, it was almost a relief—I didn't want her to get hurt as a result of my problems.

We had decided to wear all gray today because Mom feels that gray represents courage and helps with certain charms she had in mind. Who knows? She has close ties to this situation, so we had to obey, I guess.

Nurse Jen said good-bye politely to Mr. Paprika and followed us quietly out the door. She was young, pretty, and really nice. She showed me her medical bag, and I immediately felt relieved. Victoria would be just fine in her hands.

"Good-bye, Licklici," Mr. Paprika said. "I wish you a safe return."

"Good-bye, Father," was Licklici's response. We were all a little tearful.

"Bye!" the rest of us called out. We were going to walk to—well, I wasn't sure where, exactly—but then we would teleport. We needed some fresh air.

I was a little surprised we hadn't done more preparing for the spell fight. I mean, we had practiced tons of spells in the workout, but none really as a group. I guess we were going to wing it. Hey, if it got Victoria back, I was just fine with it.

We walked for a mile or so across Jupiter's rocky terrain. I had sweat pouring down my robe; it was disgusting, but I put up with it because we were on our way to *get my best friend back!*

"It's time," Mom said, pulling out her wand. We all did the same, including Nurse Jen. I felt a little more confident with the familiar wood in my hand.

"Okay, crew, we're going to say, 'Widdidorm's jail, kapah, kapah, niervo.' Say it three times and close your eyes. When we get there, be prepared for battle. Are you ready?"

I took a deep breath and fired up a prayer.

"Ready," we all responded at once. I felt something warm in my hand and looked down. It was Josh; he squeezed my hand and smiled at me, his face a little shiny with sweat. My pulse raced, and adrenaline shot through me. I smiled back; it was go time.

"One, two, *three*!"

"Widdidorm's jail, kapah, kapah, niervo; *Widdidorm's jail, kapah, kapah, niervo; WIDDIDORM'S JAIL, KAPAH, KAPAH, NIERVO!*"

I shut my eyes tight and felt the world spin. The world blurred and spun faster and faster. My throat closed, and I wanted to scream for air.

Suddenly, everything stopped. I opened my eyes tentatively and scanned the terrain. It was exactly as I had remembered it—

the palace made of black marble loomed in front of us. We were standing on its steps.

Then a figure stepped out, blocking the entryway to the prison. The person was male with jet black hair and glowing eyes. When he spoke, I realized that it was my second-worst enemy, the one responsible for keeping my best friend as uncomfortable as possible.

By the look in Jason's eyes, it was obvious that he sensed us but couldn't see us. I realized Mom's trick—she had put a charm on our clothes so that we were invisible! This trick made us so much harder to target. And it would make Jason a *lot* more vulnerable.

I reached out and high-fived the person nearest to me, hoping it was Mom. It was someone's head.

"Sorry," I whispered.

Then Jason spoke. "Well, well, well. Who do we have here?"

And, of course, not one of us volunteered an answer.

Chapter Twenty

We walked up the steps, trying to move quietly. Jason tried to appear fearless, but he looked totally unnerved. I reached into my robe pocket and pulled out my wand, hoping it was invisible, too. It was.

"Who's there?" he cried out.

Mom pointed her wand at him and raised it, sending him into the air without a word. She began walking, and he floated ten feet away from her overhead. She walked into the prison and down the hall to the one jail cell. Then I saw my best friend for the first time in what felt like forever.

"Victoria!" I cried with tears in my eyes. I ran towards the cell's door and tried to break the padlock.

I heard Jason cry three exotic words, and I knew he had done a spell to make us all visible.

Victoria moved as close to me as she could. She looked dirty and skinny, but her eyes were hopeful when she saw me. I smiled at her, and she returned it. "Twins!" I said, reaching for her hand through the bars to do the handshake we did whenever something was the same. She couldn't reach me, so I just did it myself, making her smile again. "We're gonna get you out!" I whispered, and she gave me a thumbs-up.

By now, Jason had escaped Mom's spell by using one of his own, pulled his wand out of his pocket, and shouted fiercely, "Oresp!"

Ropes shot from his wand and wrapped around me. He grabbed my wrist. I winced when his rough grasp chafed my skin.

He pulled me to Victoria's jail cell and hurled me in there. The ropes released me as he slammed the door with a bang.

I hit the ground hard, groaning. I felt tears come to my eyes and then looked around.

I could see everyone now, sizing each other up, not moving a muscle. Wait! I could still do spells through the bars of the jail cell. I remembered the exact spell I had jokingly done to Ella months ago.

"Collapserita Muscularanarium!" I screamed through the bars, pointing my wand at Jason.

He collapsed immediately. His face paled even more than it already had. I saw his chest rising with shallow breaths; it was obvious he had a third lung.

At that moment, I ran over to Victoria. I hugged her hard, and she squeezed back, though a lot weaker than me. "It's so good to have you back," I whispered. "I missed you sooo much."

"Thank you for saving me," she whispered back weakly, but smiling again.

"We're capturing Jason," I explained.

"Then just do the ropes thing. He won't be able to break out of it. It's physically impossible."

"Oh my goodness; you're right."

When Jason turned his attention to Josh, I saw my chance. "*ORESP*!" I screamed. Mom looked at me, recognition dawning on her face.

Ropes shot out of my wand and wrapped around Jason. I brought my wand closer to me, and he slid towards me, only a few feet away. He reached for his wand, but I lunged over and grabbed it swiftly from his pocket. He watched as I snapped the wand in half and dropped it on the ground, knowing that if a wand isn't completely intact, it isn't usable. He stared at it, then at me.

"You're coming with me," I told him, glee in my voice. We had done it! Now all we had to do was the spell to break Victoria's chains and we were home free.

I unlocked the door from the inside. Victoria had been a prisoner because her chains wouldn't reach the door. I slipped out, leaving it open a crack so we could get in again.

Mom did a spell to take over, transferring the ropes that bound Jason from my wand to hers. She did another spell that would keep him still for a few hours—he was frozen, couldn't move at all. She teleported him to the battle school, knowing that Gesule would take care of him there.

"You know the spell?" I asked.

"Definitely." Mom placed her wand on the wrist restraints and said the magic words. The chains disappeared. Then she did the same to the ankle shackles. And just like that, our mission was complete. *Victoria was free!*

Victoria stared wordlessly at her wrists, like she couldn't believe she had been saved.

"You're coming home," I whispered in her ear, and she grinned back at me, tears glistening in her eyes. *That* was the exact moment my stomachache—my longing for my best friend—disappeared. I gave my mom a huge hug of gratitude for helping me save her.

I looked at her wrists. They were bloody and a little twisted where the shackles had pressed into her flesh for so long. I had to look away.

"We'll get you fixed up right away," Jen said, taking her arm. Victoria swayed a little and I realized the chains had been holding her up. She needed to eat, rest, and get stronger.

"We'll see you back at the battle school," Jen assured us. Then, wrapping one arm around Victoria and clasping her wand in the other hand, they teleported.

"Now what?" Josh asked, voicing everyone's thoughts.

"I think we just teleport back," I said. "Our mission is over, right?"

Or so I thought. As soon as I spoke, a frosty breeze, chilling to the bone, drifted in through the open doors.

"Widdidorm," Mom said quietly. Josh squeezed my hand reassuringly, and Licklici gave Mom a hug. This would be the battle of my life: Widdidorm vs. Mom and me.

Chapter Twenty-One

Panic flooded my mind, feeling that creepy cold seep into the air. I felt defeated for all of three seconds before I thought, *Well, we didn't come all this way just to lose more people.*

I would not let this become a cycle of torment for his pleasure. I was going to fight back.

"Licklici," Mom directed in a quiet but firm tone, "Please take Josh and Ava back to the battle school. For me."

"No way, Lilly," she said, shooting a look at me. "I need to be here." To calm her thoughts about me, I thought. To see me fight, to know that what she had believed all along was right. And I would make sure it was a good show. This was Widdidorm we were talking about!

The air was misty and cold. Everyone was tense and anxious, not knowing what would follow this ominous air. Josh's jaw was clenched, and Mom's eyes were zeroed in on the door, ready for whatever was coming next.

I heard a loud crack, and then Widdidorm appeared with a flash of light in the doorway. His hair was buzzed, his black robes open, revealing his white tank top and black shorts. His toned stomach muscles rippled with energy. Obviously he had been using some pretty complicated charms to get this fit this fast. His eyes were full of hatred as he glared at me. For a split second, everyone was quiet, sizing up their opponent. Then Widdidorm gripped his wand like a lethal weapon and pointed it at me. I braced myself, stood tall, and faced him. My attitude was fearless. Mom was watching me closely.

"Peter," she said softly, her word like a small rebuke.

I don't think he had seen her standing in the shadows. One glance at her and all the hatred and pain went out of him. He deflated like a balloon.

He sighed, his toned abs shrinking into themselves. For a second, I thought I saw his eyes revert to a chocolaty brown. "Lilly," he said softly.

"I never thought I would see you again," she said to him quietly, and he looked down, ashamed.

"Me neither," he replied, now looking down at the wand in his hand as if it were just a stick of wood, which we all knew wasn't true. I had once heard that Widdidorm's wand had been specially crafted for him. He didn't seem to think so highly of it now.

Then Mom's tone changed—she was all business. And anger.

"You have no right to do what you're doing. You are a man worth less than I ever thought, and I'm ashamed to think that I ever loved you. What you have done to *my* daughter—my own *daughter*, Peter!—is absolutely horrible. And her friend—don't get me started. She almost starved to death, and we don't know whether she'll live after the horrors she has faced! All of the trauma, Peter," Mom said, her tone becoming almost gentle, yet dripping with disappointment. Mom still had the drama thing going for her. "You've become a monster. Or worse. I fear you're too far gone for anybody to view you as a human being again. No wonder you can't return to Earth."

More energy drained out of Widdidorm, leaving him a saggy, middle-aged man. His face colored more than I had ever seen it before, until he was almost blushing. Obviously he still had feelings for my mom, but his 'Lilly' no longer existed. Lilly didn't like him anymore, not the least bit.

The chocolate brown eyes lingered even longer, and I knew it was my turn. He looked pretty defeated already; maybe we wouldn't need a spell fight this time.

"And I have even worse adjectives for you, *Peter*," I started, making his name sound like the absolute worst word in the world. "You are cruel and destructive. And I understand your reasons for hating me. First of all, I get to be around my mom—Lilly—" I mimicked Mom's name in a funny-sounding voice, "—all the time. Second, I didn't have a horrible childhood like you. My mother, your *ex-girlfriend*, raised me with kindness and love. Third—you're jealous because I'm not lonely like you.

"I might grow up to be a scientist or something for the *good* of witches and wizards. I have *great* friends who support me, another reason you hate me. And the last thing you should know about me, before you do something irrational—which I know you will—is that—" And suddenly his wand whipped into motion, and the spell was already halfway across the room.

"Hilariationist!" my mother screamed before the spell could reach us. Her words made Widdidorm's spell freeze in midair. Pause the movie for a sec and angle on Widdidorm's shocked reaction. He must have forgotten who had helped him get this good. *Think again, Widdidorm, because my mother is as good as you—maybe better, because she's on the good side.* After this spell fight, I was determined there wouldn't *be* a bad side.

I had been watching Widdidorm's expressions during our conversation with him. For a second, the battle was paused, neither side firing spells. Widdidorm looked pretty worn down, but I seriously think he still didn't know how much he had hurt my family, especially me. But all that was going to change soon, because I was done—D-O-N-E—with him. He was wasting time that could be spent on something useful. I was especially determined because if I didn't end this now, he would continue to target my family—Agnes included—until he died. And I didn't want my sister to go through this.

Widdidorm stared at my Mom for a few seconds, hurt interspersed with the hatred in his eyes. They changed rapidly from an almost handsome brown to a fiery red that scared the be-jeebies out of me. Finally they stayed brown for a few seconds. Widdidorm spoke, breaking the silent tension between him and our group. "Why do you do this to me, Lilly?"

Mom's eyes lit up, so full of energy that I feared they might turn red like his. "Why do I do this to you!? Why do you do this to me, Peter? Why *me*!?"

His eyes focused on the floor, as ashamed as a little boy now. Good. He had a reason to be.

While he and Mom were arguing, Josh walked over to me. I was glad that *his* chocolaty eyes would stay brown forever. He took my hand and held it in his. Licklici discreetly looked away, pretending to watch Mom and Widdidorm.

We needed to hurry up with our mission because Gesule would send a rescue team if we weren't back by lunchtime, and it was already eleven o'clock.

Josh put his arm around my shoulder and let me fall into him. All the energy from the day seeped out of me and I rested my head on his shoulder, feeling his strength and sureness. I wondered if this was what Mom had felt when she hugged Widdidorm—excuse me—Peter. I had always separated the two names in my mind, even though they were the same person. I mean, there's Widdidorm, the evil sorcerer. Then there's Peter, an alter ego of Widdidorm.

A few seconds later the spell fight was back on.

"I never thought you would be this way!" Mom screamed across the room at Widdidorm. "You're so… cold!" And with that corny joke, an ice ball appeared on the end of her wand and sped towards him. The ice exploded on his thigh—that had to hurt. Then the ice spread to the rest of his body, faster than I had ever seen the spell work. Soon all that poked out of the ice case was Widdidorm's head.

"Peter," Mom said quietly, "I fear for you."

Two seconds later he miraculously broke free of the ice. The instant he did, Mom fired her second spell. "Silencoroho!" she screamed, her voice fierce. He fell silent immediately, breathing, but not moving.

"What did you do, Mom?" I asked.

"Lilly!" Licklici spoke from where she had been watching. "That is the worst form of magic. Why do you know it? Why would you use it?"

"What is she talking about?" I demanded.

"The spell is an evil type of magic," Mom began, her eyes darting to where Widdidorm sat motionless on the hard floor. "Widdidorm slipped one night and taught it to me—he learned it from an ancient spell-book. The spell silences the opponent and forces them to be still, so he can't do spells, making it easy for the spell-caster to move in quickly. Very handy. Not that I would know, as I've never used it before," she said quickly, shooting a guilty look at my headmistress. In some ways, Mom is still a teenager.

Then, striding toward Widdidorm, Mom spoke in the severe voice that she saved for those special occasions when she was way too angry to yell. "You touch either of my daughters ever again, Widdidorm, and I will find you myself and *personally—finish—you!*"

His eyes glowed with a fiery red light that softened when he realized what she had just said.

"You heard me, Widdidorm," she said, spitting out his name as if it had a horrible, bitter taste. "*Both* of them. I don't lie."

Then she turned on her heel and strode over to us.

Too soon, Widdidorm broke free of the spell, bristling with a fresh wave of anger.

But I was filled with a new wave of anger, too, and I couldn't just stand and stare at him, wondering what to do. I'm aware that I get irrational sometimes when I'm way too angry, but sometimes that's when the best spells come out.

The next few seconds played out in my brain just before they happened. Widdidorm raised his wand, and I rolled to my left just as the spell hit. The spell was meant to destroy the spot where it was aimed, so when the floor split open and a hot flare of magma rushed up to meet the ceiling in a fiery explosion, sort of like a magma geyser, I was glad I had made that move so quickly. I would've become Ava soup!

I moved behind Widdidorm, targeting the spot I would need to hit to make it hurt bad enough—where the ice ball had hit his thigh. I knew it would still be stinging and probably cold—and everything hurts more when you're practically frozen.

He advanced on me, throwing a mean punch to my shoulder. Pain exploded like millions of little firecrackers as the nerves erupted. Okay, that hurt.

But I still threw my punch. *Remember, Widdidorm, I'm not the weak girl you think I am. Never was.*

Bang. I hit solid flesh, putting as much force as possible into the blow. He jumped back and sort of held his thigh. His eyes narrowed and stared me down, waiting for me to make the next move.

Making the next move was fine with me. Hours of training with Gesule had taught me there was no problem with throwing the first spell. In fact, I *wanted* to act first. Why wait for pain if you can possibly stop it?

My sequence was timed perfectly. First, I flung Widdidorm into the air. He flailed and screamed some mighty unkind things down at us for a few seconds, and then I brought him crashing to the marble floor. His inhuman qualities actually prevented that from knocking him out. He brought himself back to a standing position and staggered a little to the right, a little to the left.

Just when he thought he was making a comeback, I hit him with one of my favorite spells. "Pyrotium!" I screamed in glee. A ball of fire appeared at the end of my wand, and I picked it up, pain free. It molded to my hand, and I thrust it forward: airborne fire! All those years of recreational softball paid off, because the ball gained on him with amazing speed. The fire spread all over his clothes.

I didn't want him to just burn to death. That wouldn't have been dramatic enough. So I threw a ball of ice and cooled him down quickly.

Now I knew exactly what he needed—a nap. He must be exhausted from this battle. I wanted to be considerate.

"Slumber-OSA!" was my last spell. And just like that—even Widdidorm didn't have resistance to that kind of spell—he dropped into a peaceful slumber.

Everyone congratulated me when I finished. I was breathing pretty hard, and I knew that I had done way too many spells for my age. Josh gave me a hug, and I leaned on him, exhausted.

Widdidorm woke up way too fast.

"Don't worry, Ava," Mom said when I stood up to face him again. "It's not just you fighting him. I got this."

"Okay."

Mom looked regal in her robes, holding her wand with an air about her that was elegant and powerful.

Widdidorm stood up wearily, his eyes full of hate. The air buzzed with tension. This standoff between he and my mom was even more intense than I had imagined. "Elarear!" she screamed, the exotic word escaping her mouth just as a spell whizzed out of Widdidorm's wand. It missed us but exploded a wall. Widdidorm suddenly looked very confused.

"What did you do, Mom?" I asked.

"Mrs. Popolis," Josh said, speaking for what felt like the first time in forever. "You are officially the coolest mom I have ever met. Battling Widdidorm, handling everything so calmly—you're awesome."

"Thanks, Josh," Mom said.

Then, turning to me, she said, "The spell makes Widdidorm deaf for a short amount of time. He can hear nothing, and the world is black and white as well. You see, Ava, Widdidorm is one of the best wizards of our time because he focuses on little details that most wizards and witches don't notice. Like the color of spells. If you went up to him and asked what color a certain spell was—you know, the color of electricity when it comes out of the wand and at the opponent—he could tell you almost every time, even if it was one of those random, silly spells. So when you fire a spell, Widdidorm knows which one it is almost before you utter the words. He recognizes it very quickly—he actually taught me to do the same. Anyway, if we put the world in black and white and make him deaf, he won't know what spell we're using, making him very vulnerable. This is when we capture him."

I was stunned, falling back for a second. I felt Josh put slight pressure on the back of my arm and I caught myself, feeling like an idiot. Why did I feel let down when we finally were going to capture Widdidorm, finish him off? Hadn't that been the goal the whole time?

He killed innocent people, I reminded myself, steadying my mind. We needed to do it now, while he was most vulnerable. I felt immense relief.

"Oresp," Mom said quietly. Ropes shot out of her wand and attached to her ex-boyfriend. He looked at her for a fleeting moment, fake remorse and repentance on his face. For a minute, I thought Mom might let him go, but she steeled herself and held onto her wand. She walked out of the prison with the most evil sorcerer at the end of her wand like a wolverine on a leash. Licklici followed behind, making sure he couldn't escape. She cautiously walked over to him and took his wand out of his robe pocket, a dangerously bold move. He couldn't fight back, though, because his wrists were tightly tied with rope that crackled with magic. Licklici then pulled her wand out of her robe pocket and uttered her first spell of the night. "Carefario," she said confidently. A silvery light descended on Widdidorm, making him glow eerily. After a moment, the light dissipated, and Licklici tucked her wand back in her pocket, a satisfied look on her face. Then she teleported Widdidorm's wand to the battle school.

"What did you do, Licklici?" Josh asked. He always assumed this polite manner and speech when he talked to adults. I thought it was kind of sweet.

"The spell is just a guard to make sure he doesn't escape. It sedates his powers," she said, grinning.

"That's nice," Josh said, nodding, and I had to stifle a giggle.

We walked for a while, but eventually I had to tell Mom I couldn't walk another step. "I'm so tired," I told her. We couldn't see the prison anymore, and I hoped I never had to visit the dreary building again.

She just waved her wand, as did Licklici, and we teleported all the way to the battle school without saying a word. I guess Mom was as emotionally drained as I was.

When we returned, we were all tired and hungry. But before we could eat, Mom had a little trip to make. She walked Widdidorm down the hall and entered a room with a door that had a security warning on it. She handed Widdidorm over to the guards, who were dressed in black and wearing mirrored sunglasses. I watched them form a box around my worst enemy until I couldn't see him anymore. Mom didn't look back once, guiding us like a strong leader to the kitchen.

"We're back!" Licklici shouted, taking a seat at the table.

Mr. Paprika emerged. When he saw how tired, grimy, and just plain worn-out we all were, he grinned. I think he sensed our feeling of victory emanating through the weariness.

"Father," Licklici said, "may I please talk to you alone for a few minutes? Let's go to the Mars sitting room."

I grinned. I love how the names of the rooms begin with a planet and end with the function of the room. Mars sitting room. Saturn bedroom. It always makes me smile.

"Sure," Mr. Paprika said, not so cold for once. "After you."

As they walked out, Licklici shot me a look. She grinned and then crossed her fingers for good luck. I did the same, and she danced out of the room, a little giddy at the thought of making up with her father.

"Your food is prepared," one of the chefs announced, skillfully carrying four plates at once. "Here you go."

We all looked at the delicious power-helping food. Then we looked at each other and dug in.

"Mom," I said after devouring the lunch of the century, "may I be excused?"

She gave me a look with her eyes, zeroing in on Josh. I knew the look plain and clear. *Help me.* She didn't want to be alone with Josh, who was my friend and not really hers.

This time, though, I ignored it. "I really, really need to go somewhere," I said.

Mom finally got it. The reason why I wanted to leave this victory meal: Victoria!

"You may be excused. Josh, are you finished? Ava might need company."

"Yep. We'll see you later, Mrs. Popolis."

And then, back to the clown he normally was, Josh took my arm in a joking way and led me down the hall. To visit my best friend in the universe.

I laughingly pulled away and sprinted towards the teleporting room. Before Licklici had left with Mr. Paprika, she had given me permission to use the teleporter by myself. "You're a big girl," she had said with a wink. "With a best friend who's been dearly missed."

Grinning, I pulled open the door, whipped out my wand, and told Josh to hurry up.

Pressing the button, I shouted, "Hospital!", hoping that it would take me straight there. The hallways at the battle school are like impossible mazes.

Miraculously, it did.

Chapter Twenty-Two

I knocked loudly on the door marked 'Patient Recovery'. Josh hung back a little, knowing I wanted to do this alone. How sweet.

Jen escaped from the room, making sure to keep the door as closed as it could be when she slipped out. "Shh," she warned. "She's sleeping."

Then I heard a voice, weak and feeble, but there. "Ava?"

"You woke her up," Jen admonished. "Well, you might as well see her."

I grinned, and Josh took a seat in the hard plastic chairs of the waiting room, similar to those of the waiting room at Dream Ring.

I opened the door with a soft *click* and padded over to the bed.

"Ain't you purty!" I said in a southern accent with my voice lowered.

She laughed the same pure laugh as always. I sighed with relief—I mean, I had been worried. I gave her a hug, so glad that we were finally together again. I pulled a chair next to the bed and sat down.

She looked… tired. She had obviously been bathed, as there wasn't a trace of the dirt and grime she had been covered in. She smelled like the breeze at Ocean Neptune, her hair still a little wet. They had cut it, probably because there had been an inch or two of grimy, matted dead ends. Her brown hair was shoulder-length now. When she talked, her eyes sparkled, back to the pretty green they had once been.

"You came back," she whispered.

"Did you doubt me?"

"Of course not, but I'm still honored. Where's Widdidorm?" she suddenly asked, her eyes going wild and unfocused for a second. I drew back a little, then went in close. I took her hand and whispered in her ear, "In prison, where he should be. To join Minaga and Jason."

Then, just as quickly as it had happened, she went back to normal. "So, what's been happening?" she asked, totally the BFF I had been missing.

"Did I not tell you?" I asked, excitement rising in my voice.

"What?" she asked, leaning forward like we used to do when the other had a piece of juicy gossip.

"I have a baby sister!"

"What?"

"Mom and Dad decided to adopt a little girl! Her name's Agnes, and she's one-and-a-half years old. She's adorable, Vic. Absolutely adorable."

"Wow. Got any pictures?"

"Yeah. Let me get it out…" I fished around in my pocket until I came to the photograph of Agnes. Her hair, her cheeks, her happiness… I couldn't wait to meet my new sister!

"Aww—she's so cute!"

And then Jen bustled in. "Victoria Mongrelo!" she rebuked in a tone that reminded me of Nurse Norah. "Rest your head! You know you're not strong enough to sit up by yourself! Ava, I'm going to have to ask you to leave. She really needs her sleep."

"No, thanks. I haven't seen my BFF in nine months, and I'm not leaving after a little ten-minute talk. It's time for some deep conversation."

"Ava—"

Then Victoria cut in. "Nurse, I feel fine. That pain medicine really helped. Please. I need Ava. I can already feel my fatigue vanishing."

"That's because of adrenaline," Jen said in an almost bored tone, studying her nails.

"I need this," Victoria insisted.

"I'm warning you. Twenty minutes more. Tops."

"Yeah, yeah."

Nurse Jen bustled out of the hospital room, pretending she had some other patients to attend to, when we all knew she really didn't.

"Oh my gosh, Ava, thank you so much for not leaving. I've missed you a *ton*."

"I know—like, it's not even funny. I'm not sure how I even functioned without you. I don't remember half of the events of this past year. I was always missing you. I had this awful stomachache that never left and my head hurt really bad all the time."

"If you didn't visit me in those dreams, I don't know what I would've done—"

Nurse Jen bustled back in, and I knew she'd been listening to us.

"Visits? Dreams?"

"Well, yeah—"

"Ava, what powers do you have?"

"Weather, Fingernails, and Potions."

"I'll be back. I have to make a call!" And with that, Jen was gone as quick as she had come.

"What was *that* all about?" Victoria asked, rolling her eyes like she used to.

"I know this is gonna sound a little crazy, Vic, but I think I have four powers."

"That's not possible, Ava. It's not normal!"

"Have I ever been normal?"

That got a smile out of her.

"I'm hot. Will you take the covers off me?" Victoria asked.

"Yeah, sure. Is that okay and everything?"

"Why wouldn't it be?"

I pulled the covers off and gasped.

Her legs were so *skinny*. The shackles had left a red ring around her ankles. She wiggled her toes and winced a little bit, like her feet were still getting used to having all the blood they needed.

"Have you eaten at all?" I asked, not caring if that sounded rude. She knew what I meant.

"Yeah. I'm really craving a chocolate chip cookie or six, but Nurse Jen said they're going to 'wean' me back onto rich food. I'm allowed to eat as much oatmeal and tasteless food as I want. I've eaten four bowls of oatmeal in the past hour, and I think I've gained at least ten pounds. Oatmeal is dense. I hope it sticks to my insides," she said, grinning as she put air quotes around the word 'wean'. "Yeah, I'm serious. She actually used the word 'wean'." I laughed along with her.

"Are you making fun of me again?" Jen asked, walking in briskly. I stared at her like she was an alien—trying to make her think that idea was completely unrealistic—until she winked. If she only knew that we really were.

"Okay, so I talked to the commissioner of powers and he needs to evaluate you immediately."

“Okay—?” I said, making it sound like a question. “I don’t know what that means.”

“It just means the man in charge needs to see you and give you a sort of magic checkup.”

“Bring it on. I have nothing to hide.”

Then I added, “But I hope this commissioner or whatever knows that I won’t leave her side, so he’ll have to come *here*.” Jen sighed, but I think she was used to my personality by now. She probably knew that I was serious, too.

“I’ll give him another call.” She sighed and left again.

Victoria and I giggled. I covered up her legs again and squished into the bed so that we were sitting side by side.

“How are you *really* doing?” I asked, the question I had been wanting to ask ever since we got back from the prison.

Victoria took a deep breath. “Ava, I truly am a whole lot better. It wasn’t too bad in the prison.” Here I held up my hand and glared at her; I knew her too well to be fooled. “Well, it *was* bad, but I haven’t suffered any long-term damage. I mean, yeah, I’m scared to death at any mention of him—” *Was she talking about Jason or Widdidorm*? I wondered. “And I won’t have my powers back ’til the start of senior year at the earliest.”

“Why?”

“Well, because powers need something to base themselves on, another source of humanly power. Like a healthy body.”

“Go on.”

"But I'm doing fine. I have an IV to make sure I'm getting all the vitamins and nutrients I need, the ones I don't get from oatmeal." I smiled. "I just need to regain weight and get my strength back. I'll be absolutely fine, Av. I'm still Victoria—there's just less of me to love."

"How much do you weigh?"

"Seventy-seven pounds."

"Vic! How could he do that to you!?"

She smiled grimly. "I'm going to be fine. If I ever need to talk about it, I'll just give you a call."

"A *call*! You know I won't leave you. Do you want to live at my house or do you want me to live with you?" I asked.

Vic laughed out loud. It really amazed me that she had made the transition so quickly from half—I hated to say it—dead, to my old BFF who could laugh and be just fine.

"We'll talk to my mom and see," she said.

"Sounds like a plan."

Just then, there was a knock on the door. It opened without waiting for an answer and two people stepped inside the room.

Jen was with the man who was obviously the commissioner of powers. He was tall and his eyes were gray, his manner serious and calm and all those other qualities I don't possess. He held an old-fashioned medical bag.

"Hello. You must be Ava," he said when I jumped out of bed and onto my feet.

"Yes, sir."

"We'll just take you to the other room and give you a quick examination of your powers and then bring you right back."

"No, sir," I responded.

"Excuse me?" I don't think that this solemn man in a lab coat had ever been told no. His eyebrows arched up high, making him look pretty hilarious, and his shoulders stiffened.

"I can't leave Victoria. BFF's orders."

He turned to Jen and conversed with her in a low voice. Then Jen turned to me and announced, "Ava, Dr. Jennings wants to examine you by yourself."

That wasn't necessary; I already knew that.

"Well, Dr. Jennings is welcome to examine me right here. My mother said I'm not allowed to be alone with strangers."

That was hardly true. But I *was* dead serious. I was NOT leaving Victoria.

"Miss Popolis," Dr. Jennings replied to me, "I really can't."

"Then this appointment can wait."

I was being stubborn. Dr. Jennings left and Jen followed. They went into the waiting room for a few minutes.

"Ava, you can leave for a few minutes if you need to," Vic offered halfheartedly, not really meaning it.

"No, I can't."

"Okay."

Dr. Jennings blocked the light in the doorway as he entered the hospital room. "We've decided to do the power test in here."

"Great."

He took a seat in the chair where I had been sitting just a minute ago.

"Miss Popolis," Dr. Jennings began, "Tell me a little bit about your powers. What do you have?"

"Weather, Potions, and Fingernails. And maybe Dream."

He asked me a lot of questions about when my powers came in and how often I use them. Then he asked, "Why do you say 'maybe Dream'?"

"Because I can contact people in dreams and really be there with that person."

"I'd like to test that out. Jen, get me some of the medicine," he said to her. She bustled out the door to get it. "I, too, have Dream, Ava."

"Mmm," I said with as much enthusiasm as I could muster, which was virtually none. This man didn't impress me at all. He was sooo boring. I could get rid of him, though.

He twirled his long, thin fingers around each other until they were coiled and knotted in a big mess. Then he freed himself and stood up, his thin, gangly figure towering over me. I stared up at him, wondering how we would test this power.

"I'm just going to give you a little sleeping medicine, Ava. I'll wait in a different room, and I want you to contact me in a dream and then disappear again. If you truly have the power, you will appear there for a few seconds."

"Cool," I responded in a flat tone, with as much enthusiasm in my voice as I felt.

"Here's Jen with the medicine. Happy sleeping!" he called, walking out of the room. He clapped Josh on the back with a hearty slap, and Josh winced and grinned a little uncertainly at Dr. Jennings. I giggled, as did Victoria.

"I want to keep my power, though," I whispered to Victoria. "It helped keep you alive, and me, too. We couldn't have rescued you without your information and help!"

"Then just don't contact him," she replied. It was a no-brainer, really. I didn't have to contact him. He would just conclude I had been making a fake fuss, and everyone would believe him.

"You're still the smart one," I whispered before lying down on the bed that Jen had wheeled in. Then she handed me a teaspoonful of foul-smelling, steaming yellow liquid and made it clear that I was expected to take it. I conked out quickly.

Jen was standing over me when I woke up several minutes later. "You were here the whole time," she mused. "How… odd."

Dr. Jennings came into the room a few minutes later. "Ava, you didn't come to me."

Jen stood behind me. "Nope. I tried and tried but I couldn't contact you at all," I lied with ease, crossing my fingers behind my back so it didn't count as a lie.

"Hmm. Case closed, then." He smiled cheerfully and left the room, looking happy to be rid of the obnoxious teenager.

Jen followed him to the door and came back, shaking her head ruefully at me.

"What?"

"Anyone who wasn't born in 1800 knows that when someone crosses their fingers, they're lying," she said, grinning.

I looked down. She caught me.

"But I watched you when you slept, as Dr. Jennings had asked me to. You didn't disappear at all, but your face *was* squinched up. Therefore, I conclude that you tried to contact someone, but not Dr. Jennings."

"Now that I think about it, you're absolutely right," I said, going with the opening she gave me. Then I turned on my side and announced, "Now, I really am going to try to get some sleep."

Jen could see right through me, but she left anyway.

Victoria pounced on me right away, saying, "Ava! How could you have been so stupid!? Crossing your fingers when Jen was right behind you!"

"I know, I know. But at least she believed the thing about contacting someone else."

"Did you try to? Your face *was* squinched up."

"No. I just had a nightmare."

"Oh. I have them all the time, Ava."

"I know. I'm sorry, Vic. I really am."

"Are you really gonna try to sleep?" she asked.

"No. Why?"

"Well, I'll be Dr. Jennings. Fall asleep and then contact me."

"Okay."

This time, I was for real. I rolled onto my stomach and closed my eyes, not finding it hard to fall asleep again.

Just as I had many times earlier, I wished to see Victoria as I was falling asleep. *Victoria. Victoria. C'mon girl. Victoria, where are you?*

And then I saw her. I was sitting right next to her in the hospital bed. She waved at me, and I wished to disappear again, in case Jen decided to come back. Then I was back in my bed, already waking up.

I said goodbye to Victoria and headed back to my room with Josh, who had been patiently sitting in the waiting room the whole time. Mom had called the infirmary and ordered me to come back to rest.

Chapter Twenty-Three

Mom was frustrated when I told her about the test that Dr. Jennings had done on me. At first, I thought she was angry that he hadn't asked permission to have the test done. But once I stopped for a millisecond to think about that, I realized that it was for another reason.

Mom knew I had the power. She knew at the end of last year, when I had seen Victoria through a dream. She had gripped my arm in despair when I went to Jupiter in my sleep; to make Mom believe me, I showed her my arm. She didn't need a test to know that I had four powers.

I sat on the silky bed in my Neptune room, waiting for her to finally see some reason. She paced endlessly, fingernails black as night.

Finally, Mom came to a stop in front of me. "*Why*, Ava? Why would you fake a test like that? He was trying to make a discovery for the good of the witch and wizard world!"

She glared at me from behind her glasses. Her eyes were full of disappointment.

"Because I didn't want to become a test subject in a science lab. I would have millions of doctors poking and prodding me, wondering how I had *four* powers. It's just one more than most people. But I'm not a 'most people'. I'm different. And I have enough going on in life that I don't need doctors poking me to make it more interesting."

She stopped pacing to get a good look at me. It was late, after dinner, but everyone who had gone on the rescue mission was pumped with adrenaline. I could've pulled an all-nighter and still been able to complete one of Gesule's workouts. That's how excited I was.

I was a little rag-tag at the moment, having been through a lot. Mom stared at me, my blond hair frizzy, my gray-for-courage outfit practically shredded from the day's events, my dirty sneakers broken in some places and my face streaked with dirt and full of energy. I didn't look as put-together as I normally did, but then again, none of us did.

"Ava, do you really think I need something extra in my life to make it more interesting? I need to be home more than any—" She stopped. Did she really need Agnes more right now? Did I not matter now that I was safe from Widdidorm at the moment?

"Ava, you know I didn't mean that. I say things… when I'm tired. I'm not myself—" she tried.

I waved my hand, ready for her to go away.

"I'm sorry. Your father is more than capable of handling our new daughter. He helped raise you, and he did a wonderful job."

I didn't say anything.

"What I meant was I wouldn't let you be poked and prodded by scientists in a lab. I would've let you take the test for the good of science and I'm disappointed that you chose not to do it correctly. If they had found out the truth, I wouldn't have let them so much as touch you. I thought you knew that."

Why couldn't she leave me alone? This mood swing—from angry to loving mother—was too annoying for me to process right now. I was still so jazzed up from the rescue mission that I felt the need to go to the gym and get my energy out. I got up from the bed, straightened my robe, and put my hair in a messy bun. "I'm going to the gym," I announced. "I need a workout."

I walked briskly down the hall and opened the door to the teleporting room. The other person in the room shocked me.

"What are you doing here?" I asked, not able to make out the face, as the hallway lights are dimmed during the late hours of the night. "Actually, who *are* you?"

For a split second, I thought it was Widdidorm. He was here to get revenge. *Double* revenge. He was here to really punish me for getting him trapped in jail. I began to tremble and look around for help. I knew exactly what Victoria was feeling when she had that panic attack in the hospital. I felt fear swell up in my throat, bursting and punching down the screams floating up in my mouth.

Then the person spoke. "Um, it's Josh. Are you okay?"

Relief came over me in waves. I dropped onto a bench in the hallway and began to shake. Cold sweat came over me. How had Widdidorm managed to creep into my head in such a scary image?

Josh walked over to me, a little uncertain. "You okay? Ava? Are you all right?"

"Um…"

He sat down and put his arm gently around my shoulders. "It's okay. It's only me."

I nodded, feeling the relief overcome my fear.

"Where are you going?" I asked, kind of surprised to hear the shaking in my voice, the tremble that made me feel little and weak.

"The gym. It's like I can't settle down. I was hoping a good workout with Gesule would wear me out. I did it last night, too. He never seems to sleep. Are you sure you're okay?" Josh looked genuinely concerned.

"Oh, yeah." I was surprised to feel tears welling in my eyes. I tried to keep them down.

"What's wrong? Why are you so shaken up?"

"Nothing. I thought you were Widdidorm."

"Oh. I talked to Mr. Paprika and he said, and I quote, 'If the man so much as moves an inch towards the door… well, let's just say that the guards all have weapons, and Widdidorm is never *not* at gunpoint.'"

"Ha-ha," I said weakly, slowly feeling my old self come back.

"Where were *you* going? It's late."

"To the gym. I can't settle down, either."

"May I escort you?" he asked in a British accent, holding out his arm. I put my hand on his forearm and he walked me to the teleporting room. The wobbly, Jell-O feeling left my legs after about ten steps. It would not be hard to wear me down tonight. If Gesule did it right, they might even have to transport me back to my room on a stretcher because I would be so long-gone. It would be a new experience for Gesule Watkins—a student falling asleep in the middle of leg exercises.

I smiled, just thinking of it. Even giggled a bit, feeling more and more like myself.

"What?" Josh asked.

"Oh, nothing. Just thinking."

"You know, Ava, you're unlike any other girl I've ever met in my life."

"Maybe that's because I'm the first girl you've ever met who was targeted by Widdidorm."

"Maybe. But I don't think so."

Then Josh bent down to kiss me and I panicked. I reached out and touched the teleporting button with my wand. The world spun, oxygen crept out of my mouth and sealed my throat, and I wanted to scream, just like I did whenever I teleported.

Josh smiled at me when we got to the gym, and I smiled back shyly. Would he try to kiss me again?

I mean, any other time I would've let Josh kiss me, but today was just crazy. I needed sleep, and if he had kissed me, I would never fall asleep.

"Hello, students," Gesule greeted us, not flinching at all, even though it was at least midnight. He was wearing robes that could've passed as pajamas but didn't look too shabby otherwise.

"Hello, Gesule," we responded.

"Shall we do legs or arms first? Or, to mix it up, abs?"

This was the closest I had ever seen Gesule to joking. I laughed to show that I appreciated his attempt at humor and said, "Arms."

"Legs," Josh said, also cracking a grin.

"Great."

He set us to work, pushing me as hard as ever. I sweated and gulped as much water as I usually did, and it all felt sort of comforting. Some things hadn't changed.

When I couldn't attempt a three-pound weight without my fingers dropping it, I switched to legs. Soon enough my legs were shaking and I felt positively weary. But I knew if I didn't push myself harder, the weariness would go away the minute I stepped out of the gym. So I went to the abdominal station.

Finally, my stomach muscles trembled, and I had to fight to keep the yawn out of my voice when I told Gesule I was ready to go back to my room. He dismissed me with a wave and a bottle of water. "This young man will escort you back."

He pointed to Josh, who was barely sweating. He had been on legs the whole time and wasn't shaking at all. His knees didn't clack together the way mine had for minutes after I had quit the leg exercises. He was seriously not tired yet.

"I'll be back, Gesule."

He walked me out the door. We teleported silently.

He joked about me being weak for the whole length of the hall. Then he stopped in front of my door. "You know, Av," he started. "I'm just kidding. Any girl that could do the arm strengthening for that amount of time—even half the amount of weight you were lifting—is incredibly strong. I'm just pumped up. I can't sit still anymore, and I might as well do something useful until I'm tired."

I grinned and opened my door.

"Good night, Ava."

"'Night, Josh. Thanks for everything. You did great."

"You did awesome. Good night."

I smiled, skipped across the room, jumped into bed, and slipped between the covers.

Chapter Twenty-Four

The next morning I went to the hospital almost immediately. I mean, I guzzled a bowl of Cheerios quickly and chugged a glass of milk for Mom's sake, but then I bolted to the hospital.

I had to see Kathryn. I couldn't believe I hadn't checked on her yesterday, and I'm sure she was miserably disappointed. My only hope was that she was out of it, so she didn't have an acute sense of time. Otherwise I was dead meat. She should've been the second person I visited—after running to Victoria's side.

But then again, last night was crazy. Victoria, a powers test, Josh… Josh. I had thought a lot about our conversations. He was really a sweet guy.

I knocked on the door of Victoria's room. I heard a rustling of hospital slippers shuffling on the tile floor and then the door opened. Nurse Jen glared at me. I guess I wasn't a welcome guest at seven in the morning.

But I had to see my girls, so I chose a different route.

"Can I please see Victoria?" I asked politely.

"She's sleeping, like we all should be," she said, bags under her eyes. Victoria was probably a difficult patient, with her hunger and odd timing for things.

"Excuse me, then," I said smoothly. "May I please see Kathryn? I thought she'd be awake by now."

"Kathryn's condition is still debatable," she said, making no sense to me. How could someone's condition be debatable? I didn't get it, but I went along with it.

"Of course. I figured," I volunteered in the awkward silence that followed her comment.

Her face expressed the fact that my comment was not appropriate for the topic. I felt like giggling but decided that calm composure was what would win her over.

"I meant to say that I figured she would be yearning for the presence of another teenage girl who would understand the debatable-ness of her condition."

This time it was almost impossible to keep the giggles suppressed. I coughed in the crook of my arm to get my little gasp of laughter out.

Jen smiled a little bit. "I'll go see if she's awake, since you seem to be persistent."

What did she mean? I 'seem' to be persistent? She should've known I was persistent from the time she set eyes on me. Gosh.

"She is," Jen confirmed, reemerging out of Kathryn's room. "And would like to see you. To discuss the debatable-ness of her condition with another teenage girl." She giggled a little bit. Then, seeing my still-serious face, she composed herself and nodded. "I mean, she is ready for you, Miss Popolis."

She headed back to Victoria's room. I opened the door to Kathryn's room after a quick knock and entered.

Kathryn was sitting up in bed, hooked to an IV. She didn't look as bad as the time she had been sick with Camota, but she certainly didn't look healthy. Her face was pale with a tint of green in the hollows of her eyes and around her mouth. She had pounds and pounds of covers on—I'm not kidding; I counted, like, twenty or so—but still appeared to be shivering. I padded into the room on my moccasins, trying not to disturb the silence and peace of the room.

"Hey, Kat," I said softly.

"Ava!" she exclaimed with a smile, breaking the ghastliness of her face. "Did the mission go well? Did we get Victoria back?"

She honestly didn't know how our mission had gone. Did she know it was the next day? What had Jen told her?

"Yes," I assured her, and her shoulders immediately relaxed. Some color came back into her face, and she sank back on the pillows in relief.

"Good, so good," she said. "How is she?"

"Better than I thought she'd be," I replied. "Up and at 'em, determined to get better. And quick."

She laughed at this, then started coughing.

"What about you?" I asked.

"I'm doing fine. I just have a little sickness." Her cough worsened and she bent over the covers.

"Are you okay? Do you want me to get Jen?" I asked, my eyes focusing on her pale coloring and the way she was fighting to breathe, trying to regain control of her lungs. What was wrong? Was she okay?

She made a motion at her throat, letting me know she couldn't talk. She was choking now. I ran out the door, nearly slipping on the slick surface of the floor. "Jen!" I cried.

She emerged from Vic's room immediately and looked at me with concern. She heard the urgency in my voice.

"What?" she asked. Hearing the strangled sound from inside the room, she slipped on gloves with the quickness of a fox and hurried into the room.

"Can you speak?" she asked. Kathryn made the motion across her throat again.

I turned away, unable to bear watching my friend choke. Then the horrible sound ended, replaced with normal coughing. I turned back around and looked at Jen, who was standing by Kathryn's bed, looking satisfied.

"Is she okay?" I asked.

"Yes," she answered. "Time will heal her sickness, although I might use a few spells to help it along. I am often against using spells to heal humans, but in this case, I am considering it. She's had it once before, and I want to help her get better."

"What? What does she have?" She could hear the frustration in my voice. Talking about this sickness but not naming it was driving me crazy.

"She has pneumonia, honey-bunches. Her coughing gives it away."

I felt relief flood through my body. I mean, pneumonia certainly isn't good, but it's better than Camota.

"Will she live?" I whispered, hoping that Kathryn couldn't hear me above the noise of her cough.

"Of course. She most likely won't be able to return to Neptune with you in a few days, though."

Now disappointment flooded through me. I had wanted her to be well enough to see Victoria and be there for our victory celebration.

"Would it be possible… if she made a miraculous recovery?" I asked, hoping there was some way.

"Maybe," was all Jen would allow.

She made sure Kathryn was comfortable and then left.

"Widdidorm's captured," I told her when she'd calmed down. Her mouth formed an O, and her eyebrows rocketed beneath her curly bangs. "Whoa! How'd you do it?"

"Hurt him with words. He was too shocked when I sprang a good sequence on him." She looked surprised, and I found myself worrying that she would be too hyped up after this news to settle down and recover from her illness.

"But enough about that," I said, expertly changing the subject. "Guess what? Josh and I might be a *thing*!"

"Really? No way!"

"*Yes*," I said excitedly, leaning closer. Then, thinking for a second that she might be contagious, I leaned back.

"He tried to kiss me last night," I admitted.

"And you didn't let him?" she asked, the volume of her voice rising in disbelief.

"Well, no. I totally panicked! And it was the same day as the mission, and I was stressed out and… yeah. We had both gone through a lot, so I think he understood."

"Where were you? Your mom's always around."

"Well, I couldn't sleep, so I headed to the gym and found him in the teleporting room. He couldn't sleep, either."

"That's *so* romantic," she sighed. "You're so lucky."

I shrugged her off. "We're not, like, going out or anything."

"Yeah, but still. It's like a movie."

Now the medicine is getting to her, I thought. She was turning way too dreamy for my liking. So I switched the subject. Again.

"We go back to Neptune in two days," I announced.

"Great. I can't wait to see everyone."

"Yeah," I said dryly. I knew she might be too sick and would have to rest at home for the summer, so I didn't want to get her all pumped up for our return to Neptune. Going home right away would be fine, though—she lived on Saturn with her gigantic family. She had everything she could ever need there.

Just then Nurse Jen entered the room, carrying a standard-looking oxygen mask. "Kathryn, it's time for your breathing treatment," she told her. "Tell Ava good-bye."

Kathryn had just enough time to say, "Bye, Ava," before she slipped on the mask.

"Bye."

I sat in the waiting room until Jen came back out. Then I asked if I could see Victoria.

"Sure. She's awake."

It was only seven-thirty, but then again, Vic probably had a weird sleeping routine with all she's been through and the odd timing of her treatments.

"Hey, Vic," I greeted her, seeing the reclined figure lying in bed.

"Hello," was her soft reply.

"Are you okay?" I asked. She looked worse than yesterday.

"Yeah," she answered. I peered closer at her. Her face was super pale.

"What's wrong?" I asked, immediately knowing that she was either upset or not feeling well.

She pressed a button on the hospital bed, and it elevated her to a sitting position. She cringed a little, since normal positions were foreign to her; the chains had made her as uncomfortable as possible.

"I'm ready to go home," she told me. "I want to be around people I know. I want to see Licklici, and your mom, and my mom. I want to go back to school, and be, like, almost normal again. But I'm not allowed to leave this stupid bed. Do you know that they're going to let me take the bed with me to Neptune because I'm not supposed to move? I have to fly home in this bed. They're going to enlarge the cellar entrance to fit it in. I mean, my chains moved me around like a million times a day. And now I'm not licensed to *move*? Like, how inhumane is that? Do you know what they told me? They told me that I have to sit in bed half the summer, just getting my strength back. Yeah, Ava.

"And then I can't even eat like a normal person. I'm only allowed stupid oatmeal. Jen said I'm allowed one cookie a day. One! Ava, do you know how much I've looked forward to this rescue? For so many reasons—one, I get to see everybody. Two, I get rid of the stupid chains. Three, I can eat regularly again. Finally. And *four*, I could finally… I don't know. There were many other reasons. I made a list in my head one lonely morning in the cell."

"I'm so sorry, Vic. How can I help?"

"Well…" She launched into another long speech, probably having been prepared in case I asked.

"You can sneak me cookies, for one thing." Here I held up my hand. "What?" she asked.

"Victoria, you know yourself you're not ready for such rich food. If I fed you an extra two, maybe three cookies, you would get sick. They have too many rich ingredients. It's not good for your system."

She glared at me, but I brushed it off. Of course she was going to have bad days after being imprisoned for so long.

"And another thing, since the first idea was *rudely* stomped down—" Another glare. "You can fix me. You still have your powers, right?"

I nodded. This was the first time in three years that I would be able to go back to school after a run-in with Widdidorm and not be a) incredibly injured; b) prescribed to bed-rest for the rest of the summer; or c) described as too fragile to return to school when I'm perfectly able. This year, I would be returning to school (it was only the beginning of second semester) and would be treated like a normal kid for the first time in the early months of the new year.

"Ava," I heard Victoria say, snapping me back to reality.

"Huh?" I hadn't heard a thing she had said.

"I was *saying*, can't you fix me with your powers?"

"No. I mean, yes, technically, I could try. But no." I couldn't believe I was saying this. I would do anything for Victoria, but I really believed that this way—the human process of recovery—would be best for her. What if I messed up and, like, hurt her?

"Why?"

"Because—" I stopped and thought for a sec. "Because I just can't."

"Why not? You're capable."

"I know, but Vic, that really wouldn't be best. If you want magic healing, go to someone who does that for a living."

"Are there such people?"

"Look, Vic, I have to go. I signed up for an exercise lesson, one-on-one, with Gesule. I just remembered. Hey, listen, I'll think about your… issues and try to come up with a solution. Remember, I've done the 'bed-rest for the summer' thing before. Being a pro, I can help you get through this, girly. Maybe we can talk to Nurse Norah about shortening your time in bed."

"Okay. Bye."

I walked out of there feeling a little helpless.

Chapter Twenty-Five

I really didn't have an exercise lesson scheduled with Gesule, but I went to the gym anyway. I was hoping that the exercise would help me figure out the answer to Vic's problems.

"Hey, Gesule." I set my purse in the locker that I had designated for myself. I normally stocked water in it.

"You seem down. What is wrong?" Today his bluntness made me smile.

"I'm fine."

"You go home tomorrow. Are you trying to squeeze in a last-minute lesson with me? Try to continue your training when you leave."

"Uh-huh. Sure. Legs, please."

We headed to the workout area, and I ferociously began working on getting stronger. Josh joined me twenty minutes later and began working next to me. I grinned and worked harder, forcing myself to go until I absolutely couldn't push any more weight with the lower half of my body. By now I'd been working forty-five minutes or so on the leg exercises alone. I hoped the spa was still open.

"Nice job," Josh complimented me, minutes after I'd told Gesule I was ready for the arm workout.

"Thanks."

"You're quiet today. Have hardly said a word. What's on your mind?"

Normally that would've been odd, for a guy to ask me what I'm thinking about. But not with Josh.

"Just thinking about what it's going to be like, going back to Dream Ring and finishing the semester."

"We're not."

"What?"

"We're not—finishing the semester, I mean. Licklici has ordered that we rest."

"For four extra months? Heck, no."

"You're going to disobey the headmistress and go to school when she told you *not* to? I thought anybody would jump at the chance to get half a semester off."

"I know. But… it's finally school… with Victoria. I've been waiting and waiting and now, you're telling me…?"

"Yeah," Josh said, grinning at me.

"No school?" I asked, just to make sure.

"No school! Hey, slacker, you better push harder—that weight won't pull itself."

"Ha-ha," I said sarcastically and picked up the pace a little.

"No, I'm serious. You didn't know that when you wait a few seconds on the weights, they get heavier? It's supposed to quicken our reflexes."

"*Excuse* me?"

"That's why I was always so impressed. Your repetitions weren't that outstanding—no offense—but you would always wait so long, unknowingly, to lift the weights. They were at least three times heavier than what you expected. But you lifted them anyway."

"Good one," I said, making it obvious that I still didn't believe him.

"No, Av, I'm serious."

Av. It was the second time he had used the same shortened nickname Victoria used for me. It was kinda sweet.

"So *that's* why every time Kathryn and I did the same weights, they always seemed to make me more tired. I just thought I was out of shape."

"No."

"So, what will you be doing for the extra summer vacay?" I asked.

"Um, hanging out at my house, eating junk food, playing with my wand, and seeing what I can do to my pet cat."

"You have a pet *cat*?"

"Yeah, to practice spells on."

I giggled. It was just so amusing to me, seeing that Josh—a sweet, edgy boy who was really funny—could have a pet *cat*. Cats are just so… I don't know… *not* edgy.

"Well, I'm gonna go talk to my mom and see what *I'll* be doing for the extra vacation. See ya." I slung my purse over my shoulder, said good-bye to Gesule, and grabbed three bottles of water out of my locker. Then I headed to the teleporting room.

"Are you *kidding* me?" I groaned, eating lunch with Mom. "Extra vacay? What am I going to *do*?"

"You're going to Grandma's for a few months," she replied matter-of-factly. "At the beginning of May, when school is out for the rest of the students, you will come home and help Victoria."

"But I'll miss the junior trip to Ocean Neptune that Licklici installed because of me!"

"I'm sorry about that, honey. I really am. But don't you think Grandma's house for months will be more fun than one trip with your school? Besides, we've already worked out the details. We're still heading to Neptune tomorrow, as planned. We'll spend a few days there, packing and socializing. But I can't be away from Agnes too long, Ava. She needs my love. Grandma is coming to Neptune to take you back to her place so I can rocket back to Agnes."

"Really!? Awesome! That's going to be *so* much fun!"

Mom smiled and said, “Oh, yes, you’ll have a great time!”

“I gotta go, Mom. Sorry—I need to pack!”

Okay, this was going to be serious fun. Grandma’s place was, like, the magical capital of the world. I’m not kidding. And Grandma and Grandpa are both magical, so we could have spell fights and everything. Awesome.

But what about Agnes? And Dad? And Victoria? I wouldn’t get to see them for months! That was definitely the worst part of this arrangement.

“But what about Agnes, Mom?” I asked later.

“Honey, she needs to get used to her surroundings and her family. You won’t be so much of a surprise if she gets used to the house first. Do you understand?” she asked gently.

“Yeah.”

I went to visit Victoria later that day and found a situation I hadn’t been expecting. Victoria was sitting up, looking much more cheerful than she had been earlier that morning. Jen had fixed her hair and Victoria was expectantly eyeing the door. “What’s going on?” I asked, totally clueless.

“Licklici called my mom and she’s on her way!” Victoria exclaimed. “She’s going to be here any minute. I can’t wait to see her—Ava, do you realize that I haven’t seen my mom in nine whole months? I haven't been able to talk to her or anything—so I'm about to see her for the first time in forever!"

"Vic, that's great! How exciting!"

At that moment, Mrs. Mongrelo appeared. I knew she had teleported by the way she heaved in breaths and had that windblown look about her. She crossed over to Victoria's bed and began weeping. She was crying hysterically all over herself, blotching up her face and everything. Her hair came out of its neat bun and she still sobbed. Her black skirt had darker black dots all over it from her tears.

"I've missed you, baby! I've missed you so much! Oh, deary, you're back! Thank God! Thank God!"

Victoria gave her mom a hug, and Mrs. Mongrelo let loose another wave of emotions. Victoria's shoulder was soon soaked with her mom's tears. Mrs. Mongrelo wouldn't let go of her. Victoria held her close and comforted her.

"You're back!"

More tears. Mrs. Mongrelo sounded like she wasn't speaking English, with all her blubbering and constant waves of sobs. I had known it would be dramatic, just not *this* dramatic.

Nurse Jen stood off to the side, trying to butt in between Mrs. Mongrelo's hysterical fits to tell her that Vic needed sleep. Jen was sort of twitchy, and I knew she was aggravated with the rise of volume. I giggled silently.

"You're back! You're really *back*!" Mrs. Mongrelo shouted triumphantly.

"Mom. Quiet down," Victoria said in a soothing voice. "I'm right here. It's going to be okay." I smiled at the happy reunion and left the room to let them have some privacy.

Chapter Twenty-Six

We packed our bags and made sure we had absolutely everything we needed. It was hardly believable to me that I was still able to walk on my own two legs after seeing—and defeating—Widdidorm. This time he was out of the picture. He was in witch and wizard jail, and no one escapes from there. They were going to come up with a great punishment for one of the worst men in history.

Victoria's bed was wheeled outside so she could say goodbye to the landscape. Then, expanding the entrance to the cellar, just as she had told me they would, they slipped her bed—and her—into the cellar. I could hear Victoria's screams of frustration. She wasn't allowed to get out—not really capable, either—so she still felt confined. The big difference was that now she was around people who loved her, fed her, and took care of her.

"Bye, Mr. Paprika!" I shouted as we got on our brooms. Then I remembered something. I dashed back into the house and ran to the teleporting room. Pressing the button hurriedly, I felt that whirling creepiness for only a second and then I was back in the gym. Gesule was standing there. He looked forlorn without his trainees. His face lit up when he saw me, out of breath from running.

"What are you doing here?" he asked in his funny accent, so unlike anything I'm used to.

"To see you," I responded. "We never had a proper good-bye." A great idea suddenly came to me. "Would you please do me a favor?" I asked.

"Yes."

Ah. Trusty Gesule. It was really nice how he would just help you without knowing what he was getting himself into.

"Can you summon someone for me, please?"

"Of course."

"Licklici."

He got out his wand, gave me a peculiar look, and summoned my headmistress. I'd always thought that Summoning would be one of the creepiest powers to have. And if someone summoned you… I think that would just be weird. I mean, imagine talking to a friend, and in the middle of your conversation, an invisible force just picks you up and magically transports you to another place. Weird, huh? Thank goodness Widdidorm doesn't possess that power.

Licklici appeared in front of us seconds later, knowing I was up to something the minute she set her eyes on me. She looked beautiful today, as always, wearing midnight blue robes with a white pencil skirt and blouse underneath. Her hair was loosely curled, hanging down her back. These past few days, my headmistress looked more content with her life; I think that was because she had finally ended the famous feud. Mr. Paprika had become more open, almost like a grandfather. He was kind and full of hospitality.

"Hello, Licklici," Gesule said pleasantly.

"Gesule." She nodded and then turned to me. "Ava, what's the deal? Because I know that you're the one responsible for this," she said, not beating around the bush.

"You're too smart," I said, smiling sheepishly.

"It's like an extra power that all headmistresses have, especially for devious, smart teenagers like you." She grinned.

"Cool. So, I was thinking…"

Then I thought, *Well, if Licklici says no, I don't want it to be a disappointment for Gesule.* "Can I talk to you privately?" I asked.

"Sure."

Gesule waved his wand over himself, and he disappeared. I trusted him enough to not suspect he was just invisible, secretly listening.

"Can Neptune host the battle school next year? I want to continue training with Gesule, and it might be a good idea for more students at Dream Ring to learn defense."

She looked surprised. "Ava, that's a decision that only the Council of Witches and Wizards can make. Normal teenagers can't make those decisions."

"I'm normal? *Yes!*" I joked.

She smiled. "But I am on the Council, so I'll think about it and cast my vote with your opinion in mind." Meaning she would vote for Neptune.

"Thanks."

"Gesule, you can come back!" Licklici called.

"Hello," he said, reappearing.

"Gesule Watkins, how would you like to become head trainer for our new fitness program at Dream Ring? It would mean a higher paycheck." She winked at him.

"I am stunned," he announced. "I will send you a letter announcing my decision. Thank you for the offer."

I crossed over to his side and gave him a hug. "Thank you for everything. I couldn't have been more prepared."

He squeezed back. "Good luck, Miss Popolis. You are a hero."

"Bye."

"Good-bye." I left him and Licklici to talk for a few minutes as I walked slowly to the teleporting room.

Licklici joined me a few minutes later.

"Licklici!" I exclaimed. "I didn't know we're getting a new training room!"

"That's what Frank, headmaster for a few months, has been deeply involved in creating."

"Your husband, like—*the* Frank?"

"Yes," she replied, a laugh in her voice, "*the* Frank."

We joined the others outside without even touching the teleporting button. Licklici just waved her wand over us and instantly we were back outside, where I had been only five minutes ago. Licklici gave Mr. Paprika a hug and he caressed her hair tenderly. I think I even heard her promise to visit.

I waved good-bye to everyone and entered the cellar of Victoria's broom. Her old broom had been destroyed when she was captured, so the battle school gave her a brand new one, no charge. I was going to ride in hers on the way to Neptune so I could assist her and finally spend some time with my best friend.

I walked in there and gasped. There was not one person, but two, already in the small cellar.

Sitting in bed was Kathryn. She and Victoria were chatting, deep in conversation about their hatred for their beds. Kat was also bed-ridden until Nurse Norah gave her clearance, from what she said.

"Kathryn!" I screamed and ran to the side of her bed. "I would give you a hug, but I don't want, you know… uh…"

"Yeah, I know. But I'm so much better! Jen said she had never seen someone get so much better in so little time! She had to let me go, or else she would've had to get an escort to take me back to Neptune, and those are pretty expensive."

"Cool. I'm so glad you're able to come back!"

"Me, too! I heard that we were going back to Dream Ring for a few days to wait for our parents to come pick us up, but since I live on Saturn, I'm just getting dropped off on the way."

"You're so lucky, living on Saturn."

"The air is weird there. And all I have for company are the fairies and my siblings, and a few normal people. But the rest *is* pretty neat."

"But you get to live on another *planet.* Do you know how cool that is?"

"Yes."

I turned to Victoria and said, "At least you're not going to have to watch everyone go to school while you're stuck in bed on Neptune. We're all going home for a few extra months of vacation!" That got a smile out of my two friends. I turned to Kathryn and asked, "So, how sick are you? Like, fever and whatnot?"

"I'm on antibiotics right now, trying to recover. My fever's gone, but I have a massive cough and a sore throat."

"How about you get some sleep?" I suggested. I took my job as head nurse to my two best friends very seriously—for the trip to Saturn and Neptune, at least.

We all decided to take a nap. My bed was mushy enough and my pillow felt incredible. Soon I dropped off into dreamland, and for the first time in what felt like forever, I slept peacefully.

Chapter Twenty-Seven

I sighed when I saw Dream Ring. It was beautiful and welcoming. It had been a while since I'd had some peace and quiet, and I had to remind myself that it wouldn't be for long. Grandma's house is always pretty crazy.

The main hall was filled to the brim with students and teachers. At first I thought the tables had been pushed over to the corners of the humongous room, but then I realized they had been banished to invisibility altogether.

There was a large banner painted in bright neon colors. "Welcome home, HEROES!" was written in paint, readable from a mile away. When we walked in, applause erupted like a tidal wave, and we were completely unable to move because of the hundreds of cheering kids around us. People offered us our favorite foods on large platters. Victoria was wheeled in on her bed and met with a roar of applause. She smiled and laughed when someone gave her a whole package of one of her favorite foods—Oreos. Finally, some rich dessert for my best friend.

"AVA!" the crowd screamed, and I was lifted into the air by a swarm of people.

"Put me down, peeps!" I screamed back, not liking the fact that if they lost their concentration on holding me, I would plummet to the floor. It reminded me of being held in the air by Widdidorm.

Thankfully, they granted my wish. I guess when you've rescued a hostage and imprisoned the most evil sorcerer in history, you pretty much get whatever you want.

Josh held my hand and looked at me with his warm brown eyes. Smiling back at him, I tried to slow my racing heartbeat. We raided the snack table and laughed together at the lavish party in our honor.

Everyone cheered the loudest for our shining headmistress, but she humbly ordered them to quiet down for Victoria. They kept it down until Licklici was out of sight, but after that there was a surge in volume.

I partied and danced and ate and ate. The celebration was fantastic—all of my favorite foods. Victoria was considered too frail to brave the party for very long, so she eventually had to leave, managing to hold on to her package of Oreos on the way out without Licklici noticing.

Finally, around two in the morning, the last of the partiers went to their dorm to gain a few hours of sleep. I made sure to sneak into the infirmary and give Victoria her scarf, blanket, and phone—the three possessions I'd asked Mom to bring me.

The items may sound insignificant, but Victoria appreciated them just as much as I had known she would.

My bed was amazingly comfortable. I slept until eleven; only then did I wake up because a face was looming over me, staring with wide eyes.

"Lordy, Lordy, Lordy!" Grandma exclaimed. "You slept longer than I *ever* have."

"What are you doing here so early? I'm not supposed to come home for a few days." My bluntness was the result of a rude awakening.

"To see my lovely grandchild."

"Hi, Grandma!"

Grandma has shoulder-length hair as white as snow that she wears down or in a ponytail. She's a few inches taller than me, and she always has good advice or a funny saying to share. And she is a spectacular witch—she knows more spells than me and always has practical ways of doing things with magic. Mom has told me many hilarious stories about trying to beat Grandma at spell fights and always losing. My grandma is one awesome lady.

"Okay, your grandfather and I were going to take you out to breakfast, but I suppose we're going to brunch by now. Get dressed, honey-bunches, because we know the best place in all of Neptune."

"Okay." She cleared out of the dorm and I got out of bed, gingerly feeling my shoulder, which hurt from my run-in with Widdidorm. Nurse Norah had diagnosed it as 'just sore', though.

I dressed in appropriate clothes for brunch. Turquoise robe—a brand new present from Mom—a white T-shirt, and black sweatpants. The fabric of the new robe was slippery, cool to the touch.

"You look lovely, dear," Grandma pronounced. "Just lovely."

I gave her a hug. Grandpa appeared outside the dorm in the hall. I'm not kidding—he just formed out of air. I stepped back in surprise and then ran and gave him a hug. He guffawed.

Grandpa is about six feet tall. His snow-white hair is combed nice and straight. He loves to have spell fights with the magical cat and take broom rides throughout the countryside. He tries to fix things around the house with tools, but always resorts to magic. He has been trying to invent a new spell, which is practically impossible. In his typical plaid shirt and khaki pants, he was ready to take me to brunch.

When I was little I thought that Grandma just liked to use strange objects, always playing with sticks and such. Her house smelled like flowers and some things I couldn't place. Now I realize that those smells were potion ingredients and that stick was a wand.

This would be my first visit to her house since I had learned I was a witch. That sounds crazy, but Grandma is insanely busy. She is dedicated to lots of organizations involving the use of magic and such; plus, I've been busy, running away from specific enemies or recovering from battles.

We went to the 'best place in all of Neptune' for brunch—the main hall. It turns out, since I returned home without major injuries and was able to capture Widdidorm, I was allowed to take meals in the main hall until I had to leave. Grandma has a funny sense of humor.

Grandma chattered on and on about her latest organization helping the poor aliens on Mars. When I asked her what an alien looked like, she looked surprised. "Why, you don't know what an alien looks like?" she asked, her eyebrows disappearing beneath her bangs.

"No."

Grandpa chuckled at my bluntness. Grandma said, "Well, there are many different types of aliens. There are some that are just witch and wizard rejects, and there are others that are like the Earthly stereotype—green and weird. Obviously there was a wizard in NASA who had an influence in the human image of an alien." She *humphed* at the thought of a wizard using his own special knowledge to influence regular people.

I reintroduced Grandma and Grandpa to Victoria when we visited the infirmary, and Josh and Mom ate dinner with us. It was nice to be back to the routines of Dream Ring.

Mom left after dinner. She needed to get back to Agnes, and I was okay with that. Grandma came to tuck me into bed around nine-thirty, like I was a little child. I hope that she knew that on a normal day, I would protest being tucked in, but I was just too exhausted to protest. I was super tired from the party the night before.

"Get a good night's sleep, dear."

"Okay."

"Extra good sleep, honey."

"Why?" I asked drowsily.

"We're leaving tomorrow."

My head rose from my pillow and I snapped back to the real world. "Excuse me? I didn't quite catch that last part."

"We're leaving tomorrow. We have a long day ahead of us."

"Mmm."

"So does your friend."

"Pardon me?"

"Your friend, our sweet, practically adopted granddaughter, Miss Mongrelo, is coming with us. Did you not know? I assumed your mother had told you."

"Vic? Coming with *us*!? But she needs medical attention!"

"We have lots of nurses on hand. Fairies are excellent healers."

"Fairies?" My mind was spinning.

"Yes. Your grandfather and I have recently retired to Saturn. It's quite a lovely planet," Grandma said matter-of-factly, like it was no biggie.

I felt Grandma kiss my forehead, and then the lights dimmed. I closed my eyes and processed what I had just found out.

I would be vacationing on an exotic planet—Saturn—with my best friend. How cool!

I hope Mrs. Mongrelo loosens her grip on Victoria long enough for us to whisk her into the cellar of my broom for the journey to Saturn!

www.dreamringseries.com

Want more of the story?

COMING SOON:

Book 4 in the Dream Ring Series

Victoria continues to regain strength with the help of her nurse, Fawn, a quirky, bubbly fairy. As she recovers, Ava and Victoria explore Saturn, which is full of unique, exotic experiences. But their trip is cut short when Ava and Victoria are called back to Neptune unexpectedly. Ava must become a leader and defend Dream Ring from a terrifying invasion. She finds strength in her friends, especially Victoria and Josh. In the fourth book of the Dream Ring Series, Ava Popolis transports her readers to an adventure-filled summer before her last year at Dream Ring.